THE COMATOSE

THE DERANGED SERIES BOOK TWO

KATE MYERS

THE COMATOSE

KATE MYERS

Book Cover Design by https://miblart.com
Editing by https://studioenp.com
First Edition 2020
ISBN 978-1-7332322-2-7 (*paperback*)
ASIN B07XTSM1W7 (*ebook*)

1

———

MAX

Almost two weeks have passed in a blur.

A blur of "Max, you have to eat," "Max, you need to sleep," "Max, she's going to be okay."

I'm stuck in this weird form of denial, this *I could have done more to protect her* state of mind. I can't seem to wrap my head around leaving her side long enough to eat, shower, or rest.

One time I lost my cool and now my dad has stopped allowing me in the room during his exams on her. I was still in shock, more so than I am now, and I might be guilty of freaking out on him quite a bit when he poked Skylar with needles.

In hindsight, he could have warned me, and I also could have probably realized he wasn't trying to hurt her. He hooked her up to an IV line, intra-something—he explained this was a means to replace the fluids in her body, to make sure she doesn't become dehydrated, and so her kidneys continue to function properly.

Her face is pale, and her cheeks are sunken. The freckle

below her bottom lip is a prominent shade of purple in contrast to the grayness of her skin.

My eyes burn from not wanting to look away, not being able to will myself from the possibility of her waking at any second. I keep thinking that if I force the thought hard enough, I could bring her back to life and out of whatever hell she's been sucked into.

I allow myself a few moments every so often to savor the only salvation I found on the day following our arrival at the cabin. Her journal.

It was tucked into her backpack, and I stumbled upon it while seeing what was left that could be salvaged. It felt like I had struck gold. But, peeking inside felt wrong, almost forbidden. For four days after, all I did was trace my fingers along the cover, where her name was written in silver Sharpie, trying to summon her back to me.

It wasn't until my dad and Quinn threw me out of Skylar's room after I freaked out about the IVs that I finally decided to indulge myself. I opened straight to the first page, and in an instant, my heart ached to see this tiny piece of her. I mean, that's totally stupid, right, it was her handwriting, and I was undone. I felt like I had gotten her back somehow, even though I had lost her twelve days prior.

Twelve long, agonizing days since we finally got to the cabin in hopes to find safety from the crapstorm brewing around us. The virus spreading quickly, claiming with no regard, and the unknown people responsible, making it nearly impossible to escape their capture. I can only assume we were one of the few lucky ones, with a safe haven to escape to, and the minimal warning from my dad. But to consider us lucky would be a leap, given Skylar's seemingly inescapable demise and Wiley being taken, not to mention all of the horrible things that happened in the process.

My gaze raced across the page and then stopped—I had to maintain self-control. I couldn't allow myself to binge or I would lose her once more, and as quickly as I found her. I made myself promise to only read a little to preserve what bits of Skylar I had left. I must have read that first line over a thousand times until it was etched in my memory.

My therapist said journaling is therapeutic, so here I am, journaling.

With that line alone, it had my mind racing in a million different directions. Therapist, therapy, journaling, the anxiety attacks, the breathing issues, the walls, all the damn walls. I realized immediately how idiotic I'd been, how selfish and stupid I was for being mean to her, for pushing her away. It's so easy to think you're the only one with issues, especially considering you have no idea what someone else has been through. I should have been more patient. If I ever get the chance, I promise I'll be more patient.

My thoughts are interrupted. "Max?"

I close the door in my head and look up. "Yeah?"

My dad stands in the doorway. He scratches near his ear and glances to the floor for a moment, trying to avoid eye contact. "Okay, so you're going to have to promise not to freak out, but we need to talk about something."

My heart drops, nausea courses through my body, and what's left of the protein bar my dad nearly force-fed me for breakfast this morning does cartwheels in my stomach. I stand without letting go of Skylar's hand.

"What's wrong?"

"That's not really a promise, so I'm simply going to stay over here, but..." He shifts slightly.

I clench my jaw in anticipation for whatever he's about to say.

"We're going to have to start artificial nutrition." He speaks again, disallowing me to do or say anything, "Sky, she's...she's strong, and she's so proved that to us, but it's been too long since she's had proper nutrition, and we're going to manually have to deliver that to her."

I unclench my jaw. "What does this entail?"

He seems to relax in the slightest, his brow unfurrowing as he starts his explanation. "It's a fairly simple procedure. There's a plastic tube that will be placed in her nose, which will go down her throat and into her stomach and will provide her the nutrition she needs while she is not able to provide for herself."

I ask the question that he doesn't seem to be supplying the answer to willingly. "So, what's the problem?"

"Well, someone is going to have to go get the supplies."

He stares straight into my soul, and I'm torn between being left alone with her with no medical knowledge and leaving her to possibly die.

It's almost as if he can read my mind. "Max, I don't know what to do, but we need to discuss the possibilities and figure out a solution as soon as possible."

And then he says the thing I've been dreading to hear.

"I don't know how much longer she can hold on like this."

My heart crumbles into a million pieces like a glass shattered on the kitchen floor, thrown into the trash only to be forgotten.

I swallow hard. "What makes the most sense?"

"Well, logically speaking?"

He opens his mouth to begin speaking, but we're both distracted by a random flash through the room.

I try to process what's happening when Dad makes his way across the room and to the window.

"Shh," he whispers.

Instinctually, I hold my breath.

We stand side by side, shoulders pressed into each other,

both peering out of the tiny amount of space he's allowing us to use to see out past the window blind.

At first, we see nothing, only the pitch-black night, the minimal illumination coming from the moon and stars, and then it happens again, something resembling a spotlight passing across the field, this time not hitting the cabin.

Dad steps cautiously away from the window, his face drooping, and I brace myself for yet more bad news.

"Someone's found us, Max."

He turns to me, his gaze methodically making its way from the floor to meet mine, as if he was thinking, processing, and analyzing that entire time. Finally, he instructs, "Get your gun, they're coming for us."

2

—

MAX

My gun is right where I left it, sitting on the stand next to Skylar's bed, or, well, my bed.

Upon our arrival at the cabin that fateful day, my room had been the closest to the door. That's the moment the blur began. I somehow managed to pick her petite body up, carry her into the house, into my bedroom, and lay her gently onto my bed. I readjusted her onto the oversized pillows, and the dark-charcoal comforter wrinkled beneath her. My whole body was tense, and my teeth had ground against each other in an uncontrollable clenching of my jaw in anticipation of the unknown.

I recall hands and a gentle voice—Quinn—trying to pull me away to give my dad space. I had shrunk into the corner and became as small as I possibly could, desperate to evaporate into nothing. I wanted so badly to start over, to start everything over. The day. The week. Our entire lives. I would have done everything differently; I wouldn't have allowed this to happen. This was my fault. It was all my fault.

I found myself repeating the situation in my head. I

replayed every moment, and no matter how hard I tried, I couldn't get it to be different. I couldn't bring into fruition a different outcome. I willed it to be me instead, but nothing worked; I was returned to this horrible reality every single time. My stomach turned, and all the unknowns surfaced. Was she infected? Would she ever come back to me? Was I next? Was Dad next?

I couldn't shut my mind off. But I also couldn't turn it on either, it was painfully stuck on the same thing over and over, her never making it through this.

My dad walks swiftly into the room, snapping me back to reality. I numbly grab my gun from the table. He shuts the light off, and Quinn follows him in, her brown hair flowing down her shoulders. She holds a gun, and I realize almost immediately that it's the one Skylar had been carrying.

Another flash of light cascades through the window and passes. Almost simultaneously, we meet in a crouched position.

"What are we going to do?" I whisper anxiously to Dad.

Quinn's hands shake, and my attention shifts from him to her to him again.

"I think we're going to have to stay put. Sit like ducks and hope whatever is out there passes. We can't leave Sky. So, our best worst case is to wait it out."

I regret the question but find it coming of my mouth anyway, "And what if it doesn't pass?"

"Well, then we fight."

I swallow hard, grip the gun in my hand tighter.

"Do you know how to use that thing?" I ask Quinn.

I know pretty much nothing about the girl. Her name is Quinn, and she's alone. Well, alone now. She was with her cousin, Cynthia, when crap hit the fan, but she turned deranged and nearly killed Quinn in a fit of rage. She had run out of the house they were staying in and down the street. Essentially that's where I found her, at an abandoned gas station on top of that SUV, surrounded by deranged people. I saved her, but I think she was still in shock for a while, maybe even still. I should have made more of an attempt to get to know her, to console her, be her friend or whatever, but I've been my own kind of zombie since we arrived. She's been kind to me, though, making sure to help Dad with Skylar, and even bringing me food and reminding me to eat.

She stood in the doorway a few days prior, startling me when she spoke.

"I know what it's like to lose people."

I didn't even look up at her, my voice crackling in response, "I haven't lost her, she's right here."

"Then maybe you should stop acting like you've lost her."

"Get out."

"What? I'm just say—"

"Get out, get out of my room. Leave me alone. You know nothing about me and have no right."

Turning to walk away, she didn't speak another word, and I didn't bother to see her reaction. Maybe I was harsh, but maybe she shouldn't have said something so out of line. She has no idea what I'm going through, and how badly I blame myself for letting this happen to Skylar. Quinn hasn't spoken a word to me since that day until now.

She hesitates but answers, "Yeah."

Dad reaches across and turns the safety off of her gun. "There's one in the chamber. Finger off the trigger until you're ready to shoot, and if you pull the trigger, make it count."

Quinn nods.

Dad motions toward the wall. "Max, you over there," then to the corner out of plain sight, "Quinn, there."

He makes his way to the side of Skylar's bed.

My heart feels as though it's detached itself, landing smack dab in my stomach, my stomach seeming to rise into my throat, and I fight the persistent urge to vomit. My pulse is beating so hard it throbs in the side of my face. I was so dumb for thinking any of us would make it out of this.

Another flash of light beams brighter. I struggle to focus, my eyes nearly bulging out of their sockets, and I'm holding my breath once more. I have to break that habit. I'll add that to the list of *Max's things he needs to work on*. Let's call it my *self-improvement* list.

Time stumbles to a halt, and I strain to listen intently, each second longer and more antagonizing than the last. My eyes fully adjust to the darkness again, and just as they do, I'm alarmed by voices babbling in the distance. I can't make out any words but identify at least two different people.

Oh shit. This is bad.

The light shines the brightest it's shone, and in a panic, I reflexively bite my tongue. A metallic taste fills my mouth.

"Doesn't look like anyone's home," an unidentified person declares.

Good, great, they think no one is here.

"No, that can't be true. Someone will be here."

Ugh, please leave. Do you really need to find out?

"I did not walk all this way to be left empty-handed."

Quadruple shit.

Footsteps.

The front doorknob jiggling.

I realize I had been biting down on my lip when more metal coats my mouth. Let's add that to the list, too.

I look to Dad, and he motions for me to stay in place, but the urge to be the first one to make a move courses through me. I find myself standing, gun pointed toward the bedroom door.

Knocking.

Oh god, oh god, oh god.

The unknown man's voice fills the space. "Keith Sinclair, we know you're in there."

3
─────

QUINN

Max has barely eaten in days. He's heavily irritable and understandably anxious. Skylar, who I am assuming is Max's girlfriend, has been in a constant state of not doing so well since we arrived.

Keith, on the other hand, has been in full-on work mode. He's tended to everyone's wounds, made sure to keep the solar panels cleaned daily, created a massive mess of paperwork in his living room, and all while being kind and welcoming to the stranger of the group.

That's me, I'm the stranger.

The stranger who is, let's put this simply, freaking out inside.

Somehow, I'm managing to stay put together, but I feel like at any moment I might implode.

In case you haven't figured it out yet, zombies are real. Or, well, some freakish version of zombies. Maybe I'm still exaggerating, but let me tell you this, these *things* are crazy, they're mad. They're angry, and aggressive, and they're us. Max once said it best: they're deranged. Lucky for me, Keith keeps a dictionary nearby, leaving me to discover that *deranged* also means mentally unsound, disturbed, demented, unbalanced, and unhinged. Check yes to all of those boxes.

Oh, and for the record, when I wandered a few words down in the dictionary to *deratization*, I was surprised to learn that there is an actual term for the extermination of rats. I guess we learn something new all the time.

Deratization doesn't really fit here, but dehumanization does. These *deranged*, they're us, except they cannot speak, rationalize, be calm, and refrain from beating the crap out of anyone in their closest vicinity.

The scariest part? It can happen to anyone. You, me, Keith, Max, A N Y O N E.

It happened to Cynthia. It happened, and I couldn't stop it, I couldn't stop her.

Keith reassures me that we are safe here, that no one knows where this place is, that the water is safe, the food is edible, and we can stay here until we figure out what to do next. At first, I didn't believe him. It wasn't until he went on and on about the solar panels, the water filtration system, and the pretty heavily stocked food reserves, that I finally was able to relax in the slightest.

I didn't understand how any of this worked, and almost immediately I regretted asking him. Keith is a man of precise knowledge. He's analytical and one heck of a problem-solver. He has a knack for details, and I see it every morning while he measures his coffee, and in the excessive amounts of time he spends going over each piece in his mountain of paperwork. And I especially saw it as he dove straight into the details of the complex but yet simplistic efficiency of solar panels and how photo-something energy can be stored in rechargeable batteries.

His explanation really was fascinating, but my eyes glazed

over, and the more he spoke, the more I was distracted by how much he talks with his hands and how I really miss my bed.

I really wanted to believe him, though. I thought we might actually be safe here. I thought I could finally slow down enough to process what had happened, what *is* happening.

But I was wrong, and he was wrong.

And as my gaze travels to the gun in my hand and across the room to Max, standing firmly in place, I swallow down the panic rising as another knock permeates the cabin.

4

MAX

The other person begins, "Oh, you're going to freak them out. Stop. Let me talk."

Dad and I exchange confused looks, and my heart decides to speed up, somehow even quicker than my normal anxiety, and I think it might thud-thud out of my chest.

Another knock.

The same person speaks, but louder this time. "Keith, buddy, it's Wiley. Are you in there? Let us in."

Quinn mutters something as Dad and I nearly trip over each other to fit through the bedroom door at the same time.

We make it to the front door in record speed, and my mind races to make sense of the situation. This isn't real, this can't be real.

Dad reaches the door first, forcing me to take a hefty step and stand behind him, eagerly waiting for what is about to happen.

"I can hear you idiots in there, let us in."

My throat tightens around the words fighting their way out of my mouth. "It's him, it's really him."

Without even giving me a chance to process this information, the door is open, and Wiley has one arm around me and one arm around my dad, and we're all smashed together in one huge hug, and I'm so overwhelmed with emotions and I'm so thankful and relieved, and then the realization of Skylar's condition hits me like a freight train, and I can't resist the tears anymore.

Wiley laughs. "Max, ahh, buddy, you were that worried about me?"

A man comes from behind Wiley. "I hate to break up this reunion, but I'm dying of thirst. I'm guessing you have uncontaminated drinking water here?"

I wipe my face with the back of my hand. "You're the guy, the guy from the warehouse."

"Yes, sir." He extends his hand. "Alexander Sanchez." His grip is firm and strong, and his dark eyes don't break contact with mine as he clears his throat. "That water?"

Dad interrupts, "Right, right, yes. We have water, right this way. We have a state-of-the-art filtration system fully capable of removing any contaminant with a carbon activated..." His voice trails off, and they turn toward the kitchen.

"Where's Sky?" Wiley asks enthusiastically.

I take a deep breath and face him, surveying his face as he realizes something isn't quite right.

"Oh god, no. No. No, don't tell me she's..."

"She's here."

His eyes blank. "I don't understand."

A million words try to form in my head, and I choke them all down.

"Wiley, something happened. We don't really know what it is yet. But, she's here, she's..."

"You're not making any sense, Max. What happened?"

I let out a deep breath. "The day we got here, the driveway had washed out."

"Yeah, we had one hell of a time with that. Sorry, go ahead."

I raise my hand to my head and dig my nails through my hair.

Shuffling from behind both startles and reminds me that Quinn is here.

She conveys in a hushed tone. "I don't mean to interrupt, but maybe it's best if I talk to Wiley?"

She strides from the bedroom and extends her small hand to him. "Hi, I'm Quinn. I know this is a lot to take in right now, so I'll be quick and go over the basics. Skylar seems to be in some degenerative unconscious state. Keith and I have hooked her up to IVs and are doing around-the-clock monitoring of her progress, but we haven't been able to really figure out what is happening, why it's happening, and how to help her."

Wiley's eyes widen, but he remains quiet.

"Keith and I have determined that Skylar will need artificial nutrition soon if her current condition does not improve drastically, in order to prolong her life."

"Can I see her?"

"Yes, of course, she's right in here."

I follow closely behind as we make our way back into the bedroom. Laying his eyes on Skylar, Wiley clasps his hands over his mouth. He's at her side immediately. He reaches down to move a strand of hair out of her face and murmurs, "Oh, Sky, this kills me to see you like this."

My hand finds its place to rest on his shoulder. "I'm so sorry, Wiley."

He turns to me with tears in his eyes. "You didn't do this."

"I can't help but feel like it was my fault."

"I know you would have never let this happen if you could control it. I know you love her, too."

And with his few words, all the pieces of me break all over again.

Quinn resumes, "We know no known cause of her condition, which leaves us unable to properly treat her. There seems to be some possible correlation with the water contact, but we have yet to be able to determine anything sound."

"What do you mean, water contact?"

Quinn looks up at me momentarily, almost asking for approval, or maybe offering an apology for what she's about to say.

"There was a...situation on the day we arrived. Like Max said, the driveway was out, so we had to continue on foot. We crossed the creek, and Max and Skylar we're unable to successfully cross without completely going under. They got to the embankment, but Skylar was weak and showing signs of fatigue. Her symptoms quickly escalated, and before we reached the house, she had become unconscious. Her vitals have remained weak but consistent."

"There has to be something we can do," Wiley intervenes.

Dad and Sanchez enter the room.

"This is what I was telling you about." Dad motions toward Skylar.

Sanchez hands Wiley a glass of water. "Here, drink."

Wiley reluctantly takes the glass. "Keith, you're the smartest man I know, you have to fix this."

"Although I appreciate the compliment, I'm not a doctor. Luckily for us, Quinn was in her second year of medical school, but there are only so many tests we can run here."

I had no idea Quinn was studying to be a doctor, and I can't help but suddenly feel guilty for not making more of an effort with her when she was trying to help all along.

Quinn begins, "We have limited supplies, and this poses our biggest issue in helping her."

The words are out of my mouth before I know it, "I'll go."

"Now, now, we need to discuss this. No running off unprepared," Dad interjects.

"How long has she been in this condition?" Sanchez questions.

"Roughly twelve days," Quinn clarifies, matter-of-fact.

"Interesting."

Everyone turns to glance at Sanchez, as if he may offer some kind of advice or input.

"I've seen something similar to this before. You probably have, too, if you knew where to look."

Wiley becomes more alert. "Wait, is she? Is she one of *them?*"

All business, Sanchez explains, "It's possible, although each case seems to be different. I've never known one to hang on this long, but I've also only seen..."

I cut him off. "No, she's not like them. She's shown no signs of aggression, she's been *unconscious!*"

Dad places his hands on my shoulders and breaks my concentration. "Calm down."

"How am I supposed to *calm down* when he's saying she's *deranged?*"

Sanchez shakes his head. "Is that what you're calling it? Anyway, no, that's not what I'm saying. She's not deranged, she's... I guess we don't have a name for it yet, but there are different ways this virus is impacting people."

Dad appears as if a lightbulb turned on above his head. "So you're saying there are different strains?"

"Exactly, so far, there are three."

We simultaneously ask, "Three?"

"Yes, three. The *deranged,* as you're calling them, the people in this condition," he points to Skylar, "and the mind-controlled."

"Mind-controlled?"

"That was the goal all along, until something went wrong."

5

———

MAX

We are all sitting around the table, Quinn to my right, Dad to my left, Wiley and Sanchez across from me. It kills me a little every second I'm not next to Skylar, and I fight to keep myself planted in the seat. Dad called a *meeting* of sorts, so we could all try to get on the same page.

"I just think it's best to be transparent with information at this point," Dad pleads.

"Sir, if you'll forgive me, it would take far too long to fill you in on every detail," Sanchez replies. "Perhaps, more of a need-to-know basis would suffice."

I can't help but feel like he's hiding something. His close-cut hair is lined precisely; everything about him screams military or police of some sort.

Dad shakes his head. "Could you at least tell us who, what, when, where, and why?"

"This has been forming and coming into fruition for quite some time. These *men* are somehow more organized and seem to be more powerful than any other organization out there, including the government. The founding members are unknown, and the population of their organization is also unknown, along with the headquarters, if there even is one. They call themselves *The Reformation*, or individually *The Reformers*."

A collective silence fills the void.

Sanchez takes a small breath, clearly annoyed with having to give us this information. "That answers your who, now on to the what. *The Reformation* was able to fabricate some type of mind-controlling bio-weapon as a means to gain control over the population. Over the last few months, they have been targeting easily to infiltrate cities. Columbus, Ohio, being one of those cities. The goal was to mind-control the population and essentially have all available resources for themselves."

Sanchez readjusts in his seat, appearing strangely uncomfortable all of a sudden.

"That should cover your who, what, when, where, why."

He looks at each of us in the eye, one at a time, waiting for some type of response.

Dad stares blankly at his fingers and then to Alex. "Do the cities Houston, LA, Seattle, or Denver mean anything to you?"

Sanchez's eyes flash to Dad. "Yes, sir, why?"

"I found them, along with a few others on some paperwork I stole from DimChem."

"Those were the cities I mentioned earlier for being weak to this type of attack."

"It was the water supply, right?" Dad continues.

The rest of us sit dumbfounded, either biting their nails (Quinn), rolling an invisible ball of lint between their fingers (Wiley), or nervously bouncing their knee up and down (me).

"That was one phase, yes."

"There were multiple phases?"

"Seasonal flu shots were also contaminated in most areas."

"Okay, so if I'm understanding this correctly, this group, *The Reformists*."

"That's another word for them," Sanchez interjects.

"They fabricated a virus, to use as a bio-weapon, to gain control of the entire population, for personal gain, and were able to contaminate public water supply *and* tamper with vaccinations?"

"Yes, sir."

"I can't even begin to wrap my head around how that is possible."

"Sir, I told you, they are a very powerful organization."

"Okay, well then, tell me this, what went wrong, what happened? Because if I'm not mistaken, we're not mind-controlled, and neither are those crazy people beating other people to death."

"You are correct in this assessment, sir. What happened is where I am drawing a blank. Something went wrong with the virus, and instead of there being one strain that produces the desired mind-controlled effect, there are the deranged, the mind-controlled, and those in Skylar's condition."

My stomach tightens, and I can't fight the urge any longer. I sit forward in my seat, elbows rested on my knees, still bobbing up and down. "I need to check on her."

It's as if I'm unheard when Dad recalls, "The chemicals being used to produce the bio-weapon are highly unstable and have a high risk of failure, or, well, catastrophe, once used together. I ran lab work against the vials the men in black were forcing us to fabricate, and the redacted report, even though incomplete, proved that whatever they were forcing us to make was not good, not good at all.

"I had the report in hand and was going straight to my boss to tell him I wasn't wrong and show him the facts, so he would believe me. I couldn't believe it myself, seeing him there. Lifeless." His voice trails off. "I knew something really bad was happening and that maybe he was wrapped up in it himself. I had to get out of there."

Before I can even control my body, I'm standing, and words are coming out of my mouth. "I'm going to check on Skylar."

Quinn reaches forward and touches my forearm. "I'll go with you."

I jerk away and find myself holding my forearm with my other hand, trying to rub away her touch. I have to immediately remind myself that she poses no threat, she's only trying to help.

"Sorry, I'm a bit jumpy."

"It's okay." She maintains her focus on the table.

"You two go check on Sky; let me know if you need me. We're going to continue to talk; I have more questions for Sanchez," Dad orders, motioning toward Sanchez.

"I'm just going to sit here and pretend like I'm not holy-shitting to everything being said," Wiley chimes in.

I cross the threshold to my bedroom and immediately notice Skylar looks paler than she already had become. My heart drops, and I'm by her side in a flash. Quinn fumbles with her IVs and takes Skylar's blood pressure.

"She needs nutrition," Quinn acknowledges in a small voice. "It's not a permanent fix, but it's the only thing I can think of to prolong whatever life she has left so we can figure out what's happening to her."

"What do you need?"

Her eyes meet mine. "I know the basic supplies, but we need to get them at a hospital or clinic of some sort."

"Okay."

"What do you mean *okay*?"

"There is an after-hours urgent care clinic in the next town. I'll go."

"You need to talk this over with Keith."

"Fine, I will, but he's not going to stop me. I won't let her die, not like this."

6

KEITH

There is this gnawing uncertainty, all the unknowns bubbling into this mess of a puzzle I can't quite seem to figure out.

A highly organized group of men has fabricated a weaponized virus to take over the population. To control us. To manipulate and use us for their personal benefit. But it didn't work. Their plan partially failed because the virus mutated in some capacity and impacts individual people differently than they anticipated.

I need to figure out why.

The why to the failure seems to be because the chemicals were highly unstable, that part is obvious from the redacted report. But the why the virus is impacting certain people differently is still unknown.

We are aware there are three strains. The deranged, the mind-controlled, and because of the symptoms, let's call the last group the comatose. Are there other strains that we are unaware of? We have to also consider us—we are unaffected. Are we unchanged because we are immune or because we have not been contaminated?

In regard to contamination, it seems the mediums used are the public water supply and vaccinations. That explains why the radio broadcast said to come in to receive the vaccine—they were targeting those who had yet to be contaminated. We skipped our flu shots this year, partially due to the inconsistent ineffectiveness they pose, not to mention how busy I got with life and simply forgot. The majority of people in the United States vaccinate, so it's safe to assume the majority also has been infected with this virus. As for the water supply, well over three-quarters of the United States uses public water, so it's also safe to assume those people were infected, too.

I'm a stickler about clean drinking water, though, resulting in us not consuming tap water. We have a whole house water filtration system that reaches Wiley's house, too. Because we live in a duplex, our homes are connected, and our basements are only separated by a door. It was a no-brainer to split the cost. All we had to do was get an extension on the unit and run the system on his end, too.

Based on everything I've speculated, I'm going to assume that we have not yet been contaminated.

Another thing to consider is the rate at which symptoms develop. There have been reports for a few weeks now covering the flu virus that has been rather out of control. Is it possible that this group spread a flu strain to get people to come in to get a 'vaccine' which contained their virus? Or were the symptoms from the flu strain epidemic a result of the virus spreading?

Continuing to come one after another, the many unanswered questions fill my nagging thoughts.

I need to talk to Quinn about her water consumption, whether or not she was contaminated in any way, and if she was, I should start monitoring her vitals to see if any symptoms develop. Now that I think about it, I should check all of our vitals and keep a record of any changes. I should draw blood, too. Check for any inconsistencies or similarities that might shine a light on what is happening, and if there is anything I can do for Skylar.

I'm worried about her, and I'm worried about Max because he's worried about her. I've known Skylar her entire life, she's like a daughter to me. She and Max were thick as thieves when they were kids—they grew up side by side, often eating the same meals, going to the same parks to play, taking naps in the same bed. They were inseparable, hell, Max's first word resembled something along the lines of "Ky".

Unfortunately, divorce changes people. It changed her parents, Arlo and Sophia. Arlo had a problem he wasn't capable of dealing with, and Sophia rightfully hit a brick wall one day and wasn't able to put up with his drunkenness anymore. I tried my best to stay out of it, although the few times that Maura brought a sobbing Sophia into our house with a busted lip or bruises lining her arms, I nearly lost my mind. I like to consider myself a fairly rational, calm person, but when you involve a man hitting a woman, or their child, I lose all sense of rationality.

I couldn't wrap my head around why she stayed with him as long as she did, but one day she finally kicked him out. That was the same day she told us she was selling the house, luckily to Wiley, but still, she and Sky were moving across town to be closer to her mother. I was elated and proud of her for finally making the decision to stand up for herself, but in all the chaos of this empowering moment for Sophia, I failed to realize it meant Max would lose his best friend.

He's finally starting to get her back, even though they fight like cats and dogs, and I can't let him lose her again. I can't let any of them down, not Skylar, not Max, not Wiley.

I need samples; I need blood samples from all of us, and all of *them*.

We're going to have to get the live bodies of a deranged, comatose, and mind-controlled.

And we need to do it fast, before time runs out and we lose Skylar.

7

———

MAX

Dad walks into my bedroom and announces loudly. "We need a plan. We need actionable steps to move forward with this whole situation. And right now, I need bodies."

Quinn is the first to speak up, which is new and out of character because she's usually so soft-spoken and tends to blend into the background. "What do you mean *bodies?*"

His face tenses, and he shuffles into the room to give space to Wiley and Sanchez, so they can file in, too. What was once a decent-sized bedroom is now overflowing with people.

"Yes, bodies. In order for me to hypothesize any of this, I need blood samples from all known strains. I would also like to gather samples from all of us, given I have consent."

Dad scans the room and focuses on Sanchez as he begins to speak.

"And that, sir, is why you are a valuable asset for *The Resistance.*"

A collective shift in the room allows all of the attention to be on Sanchez. He seems to have this effect every time he speaks.

"Excuse me?" Dad challenges.

"I don't want this to make you uncomfortable, sir, but you are known to be one of the most intelligent chemical engineers on this side of the Mississippi. And because of this, we are relying on you to assist in figuring out how to fix this mess we are in."

"How is that even pos—no, never mind, we can talk about this later." Dad shakes his head.

I cut in, "Quinn said she knows what supplies Skylar needs. There's a clinic in the next town, and I'm sure there will be at least a deranged or comatose if we look hard enough. I'm assuming the mind-controlled will be the most difficult to find, but we have a decent start there. I'm volunteering to go, and no one is going to talk me out of it, so don't even try. Don't even try to guilt me about 'leaving her side' because I'm already feeling it heavy, and I'd feel it even heavier if I wasn't the one to get this stuff for her."

I look from face to face, expecting some type of opposition —Sanchez is the first to speak.

"I agree with you, and I'd like to sign up for this mission, too. And from the sound of it, Quinn is knowledgeable in what supplies are needed, so I'm volunteering her, too. Between her, me, and you, we should be able to get the supplies and find a body or two."

"I'm in," a soft-spoken Quinn in the corner confirms.

"Good," Sanchez adds.

Dad rubs his temples. "I don't like this, I don't like it at all. Max, well, you're my son, and Quinn, you pose to be quite resourceful to Skylar."

"All the more reason why I should be the one to verify the supplies are correct," she commands, growing more confident.

"Yes, I know, but, you're both *children* and I don't..."

"Sir, with all due respect, you should have a bit more confidence in my abilities. I think you have forgotten that my small team was able to clear out an entire building and rescue this *child* right here." Sanchez punches Wiley lightly in the arm. They must have developed some type of rapport during their journey together. "Not to mention, I was able to single-handedly get him here safely."

"Okay, Okay, sorry, this is all just...so much."

"I understand, sir. But it appears Skylar has needs, as do you, and it seems vital to our progression here that we follow through with this mission."

"All right, I understand, but everyone needs to get some rest. This happens tomorrow. You two," he points to Wiley and Sanchez, "must be hungry. Let's find you some food, and while you're eating, I'll make your beds."

"Thank you, sir."

Walking from the room, Wiley pats Keith on the shoulder, saying, "Thanks, Dad," and they both laugh.

A few moments pass, and I feel obligated to break the silence, "Thank you for volunteering, you didn't have to."

"I know, but I want to. And it makes the most sense. It would have either needed to be me or your dad, and he clearly needs to stay here. Plus, and I don't mean this to sound as bad as it's about to, but I'm expendable."

It was then that I broke my fixation on Skylar's hand in mine and looked up to Quinn, tears forming in her eyes.

"Don't say that. Listen, I'm sorry that I've been such a jackass lately. I've been selfish, and I've been cold and shut off and punishing everyone around me for what happened to Skylar, as if it was somehow someone else's fault other than my own."

"I don't think it's your fault, Max, you didn't do *this* to her. And I don't think you realize that I understand. I'm not mad or upset about how you're reacting, it makes sense...and I wish there was more I could do."

"That doesn't make you expendable, though. That's not why you're going and my dad isn't."

"It feels that way. Not because any of you have made me feel that way. I just, I don't know, I don't really feel like I have much more to live for, if that makes sense."

"Yeah, it makes sense."

"And I know it's stupid and doesn't really matter, but I had no chance to save Cynthia. I feel like I can somehow redeem myself if I can help Skylar. Maybe I won't feel like my life is so meaningless."

"Cynthia was your cousin?"

Quinn shifts uncomfortably, her gaze darting straight to the floor, her hands weaving in and out of each other. Why is she so fidgety all of a sudden?

"Yeah."

"Why do I feel like you're lying?"

Quinn takes a deep inhalation, breathing deeply out of her mouth before she focuses intently on me, fighting the tears from making their way down her cheeks. "Cynthia was my girlfriend."

8

____

MAX

Having your cousin die is one thing, but having your girlfriend turn into a deranged zombie and try to beat you to death is another.

My brain is in such a fog of doing its best to put all the pieces together, and then the recognition dawns on me.

"Was she, was she there, at the gas station?"

"Yes."

The realization hits me like a ton of bricks. "Oh god, did I...?" I can't finish my question.

She presses her lips together, squinting and obviously trying everything she can to stop the uncontrollable tears as they come. "Yes, I think so."

I'm such an idiot.

"I-I-I don't even know what to say."

"You didn't know, you didn't mean to. You were saving me."

"I'm so sorry, Quinn, I had no idea."

An awkward silence fills the space between us, and the heavy blanket of guilt I carry seems to become weighted even more.

I press Skylar's hand against the side of my face and hold it gently but firmly between both of mine. I close my eyes and rejoice in what is left of her scent—that subtle mix of lemon and lavender.

Quinn regains her composure and begins, "I couldn't afford to stay on campus, at OSU, but Cynthia got a scholarship for basketball, so she stayed on campus. It sucked, really bad, being apart. July thirtieth would have been our third anniversary."

"Why did you tell us it was your cousin?"

"I don't know, knee-jerk reaction, I guess. It was our common excuse when we didn't think people could handle the whole 'being gay' thing. I didn't know you guys, so I didn't know how you would handle it. I'm from a small country town, and you know how those types of people handle these types of things."

"Yeah," I respond, not really sure what else to say.

"I have to admit that I had to bite my tongue and not laugh everytime Skylar kept getting blatantly jealous, like, girl, if you only knew." Quinn lets out a small chuckle.

"Yeah, she's crazy like that."

"I can tell," she laughs.

Needing to clear the air, I say, "Just for the record." I look her directly in the eyes. "We don't care, not about that stuff. So please don't feel the need to hide from us. We're not judgmental when it comes to sexuality. My dad might judge you for drinking Pepsi over Coke but not this." I laugh and then add, "I'm sorry that you felt the need to lie like that."

"Thank you," she mutters.

"And now I feel even worse. You've had to deal with *us*, and you've already been through so much more we weren't even aware of. I really am so sorry, Quinn."

"It's okay, I'll be okay. Thank you." She trails off then starts to speak. "Please let me help you, I want to make this right, I want to bring her back to you."

"That would mean more to me than you will ever know."

We share a pained smile.

I add, "I won't be able to say sorry enough. If you ever need or want to talk, I'm here. My dad is a great listener, too."

She laughs a little. "Your dad is a great everything, that guy is brilliant. Dude makes the best pancakes I've ever had, not to mention he's probably going to save us from an apocalypse."

"God, I hope so." I laugh with her.

Dad enters the room with purpose. "Nice to see the mood has changed in here, kids. Were you talking about me?"

"As a matter of fact, yes. Quinn said your pancakes are gross and she's refusing to eat your food."

Dad shoots her such a scornful look, and she scowls at me.

"I totally did *not* say that! He's lying. You make the most insane pancakes, Keith. Will you please adopt me?"

"I'm hurt. I don't know how much more of this abuse I can take," he jokes. "But hey, on a serious note, to bed with both of you. We have a big day ahead of us tomorrow and we all need to be rested. Go brush your teeth and then lights out."

"Fine, fine."

Taking her leave, Quinn utters, "Goodnight, Max. Let me know if you need me."

"Thank you, Quinn. Goodnight."

Dad walks farther in, speaking lower so his voice doesn't leave the room. "That was a nice change between you two."

"I agree. And I want you to know I apologized to her for being such an ass lately. She doesn't deserve that."

"You're right, she doesn't. I'm glad you two had whatever epiphany that you did. Quinn seems to be a great addition to the team."

"Dad, there's something I want to tell you. It's probably not my place, and it doesn't even matter, but I thought you should know anyway."

His eyebrows furrow. "What's wrong?"

"Quinn is gay."

"And?"

"What do you mean 'and'?"

"I just mean like, it's obvious." He laughs. "That's what you wanted to tell me?"

"Cynthia, the girl she said was her cousin..."

"...Yeah?" Then the lightbulb turns on. "Oh no, no, you're kidding me?"

"No, it was her girlfriend." I hesitate before finishing, "And I shot her."

"You can't blame yourself for this, Max, it isn't productive."

"I know, Quinn and I have already been over this. And as much as both of you say it isn't my fault, it's still going to feel that way. I feel terrible for her. I can't imagine what she's going through."

Dad adjusts some of the lines running to and from Skylar's IV. "I'm sure you can imagine."

"Yeah."

"Poor Quinn. This makes sense of why she's acting the way she is. Everyone loses a piece of themselves when they lose someone they love."

He's speaking from experience. Of my mom. The love of his life.

His hand finds its way to my shoulder, his grip firm, reassuring. "We'll figure this out, Max. I won't stop without putting up one hell of a fight."

And somehow, I believe him. Not only about Skylar, but this entire situation. Dad will figure something out, he always does.

After he leaves the room, I sit on the side of Skylar's bed, tucking the same strand of honey-colored hair that keeps managing to find its way down her cheek. I lean in close and whisper to her, "I know this is stupid, and I keep doing it every night, talking to you. But I need you to know that I'm here, and I know I promised to stay by your side, but I'm going to leave for a little bit tomorrow. I have to. You're not doing well, Skylar. And we have to get some things to help you. I won't give up on you, not now and not ever. Please hold on for me, don't leave me. We're going to make this right. I won't stop until I've done everything I can to bring you back to me. Please believe that."

I finish my nightly *talk to Skylar like an idiot* session and settle into the recliner my dad brought into my bedroom on the second night being here. He knew I wouldn't sleep anywhere else, so he brought in his 'favorite chair' for me to sleep in. He gave a thorough lecture on keeping it clean and taking good care of 'her' and then threw a blanket down and told me it was my new bed. And that's what it's been for the last two weeks.

My eyes, heavier than I realize, shut against my will. I struggle to stay awake, fighting my consciousness and the internal battle I have over whether leaving Skylar tomorrow is the right decision. It's the only thing I can do to help her right now, and no matter what risks prevail, it's what I have to do.

9

———

MAX

We eat a quick breakfast, because Dad insisted, and begin to say our goodbyes. My stomach tightens, knots forming over and over until I find myself hoping I don't puke up the tiny amount of toast I choked down.

I hate leaving her.

But I hate being useless and doing nothing to help her.

If I stay, it's for selfish reasons. If I go, it's still selfish, but in an effort to help.

I have to somehow make this right; I have to bring her back.

"Promise me you'll be safe?"

I stuff a sweatshirt in my backpack and turn to my dad. "Promise me you'll keep her alive?"

"Max, you know I will do everything in my power."

"Then so will I."

Sanchez stands taller, clearly showing his dominance. "Sir, I assure you, we will return by supper."

Wiley hugs me, tighter than my dad's hug, and whispers in my ear, "Thank you for this."

I give him a reassuring squeeze and say to the group, "We good?"

"Yes, sir."

Quinn offers a somber smile.

My gaze lingers on my bedroom door before I turn and walk out the front door, leaving behind my heart in a tattered mess on the floor. I bite down on the inside of my lip, simultaneously grounding and telling myself to keep it together.

"Right this way." Sanchez points toward a path in the trees, the direction we saw the lights the evening they arrived.

He continues, "Like I stated this morning, we have a brief walk through this wooded area. We should reach the vehicle in a matter of a few minutes."

Quinn pipes up for the first time since we started on this journey. "Why did you leave it?"

"Ahh, the terrain wasn't travelable, and we didn't want to take any unnecessary risks at that point."

"The bridge was out when we came through," I add.

"I think they came from a different direction, didn't you, Sanchez?" Quinn questions.

He begins to speak, but I interject.

"There are two entryways on the property."

"Oh, that makes sense."

I find myself speaking, unable to stop. "How do you know so much about what's going on?"

"Excuse me, sir?"

"You just seem super official, I don't know. I'm sorry if I'm overstepping, but you're incredibly knowledgeable about what's happening."

Sanchez responds, "I understand, sir. I'm military, or, well, ex-military. Honorable discharge."

"How does that translate to you knowing what's going on, though?"

Quinn stumbles over a branch, nearly falling down, and I reach out to steady her.

She mouths, "Thank you."

Sanchez speaks, "I'm uncomfortable speaking in this capacity. I have already briefed your father on the questions he posed and would rather we discuss this at a different time and place. You never know who's listening." He motions to the landscape around us.

And with this, I'm the uncomfortable one. I don't know why it's hitting me right this moment, but why do we trust this guy? We know next to nothing about him, mainly that he brought Wiley to us, and is 'military.' My heart beats harder, thudding loudly in my ears. My mind races, and just as I'm about to lose my cool, Sanchez speaks again.

"We have the same enemy."

Quinn states, "The enemy of my enemy is my friend."

Sanchez lets out a small laugh. "Yes, ma'am, that is correct."

We walk in silence farther from safety, I assume either with our own thoughts or from focusing on the terrain, maybe even a little of both. I still can't help but feel like Sanchez is hiding something, and maybe it's none of my business, we're all hiding something. But will his something hurt us, put us in danger? Will it stop us from helping Skylar?

I have to believe I'm overreacting, that I'm thinking way too much into this, because he rescued Wiley, and why would he have done that if he was going to hurt us? Why would he offer my dad information and offer his own resources to support us? Maybe he only helped Wiley to get to us, to get to my dad. He did say that my dad was known to *The Resistance* to be a great chemical engineer. What does he know that we don't, though?

All this thinking about who Sanchez might be or his intentions has me questioning my dad, and myself. I felt so oblivious about Quinn when she told me a bit of her truth, and I'm sure there's so much more to her than we know. Maybe there's so much more to all of us that we haven't said.

I killed a child. I know I've killed more than this one child, but I keep coming back to her, to the girl who was still in grade school, helpless but violent and deranged. She will never know her future, and although I understand the virus is what took that from her, I can't help but feel like it was my fault for making it so certain. I had no other choice; we couldn't get away. It was them or us, and Skylar and I both had to make that decision.

I'll never forget that moment, feeling the weight of the trigger, the sound of the gun crackling through the air. Seeing her body hit the ground as the life left it. Falling apart with Skylar's arms around me, doing her best to hold me together.

She promised me she wouldn't tell them what I did. I don't know why I made her promise, but she did. Maybe because if I spoke about it, if I told my dad and Wiley, it would somehow make it more real, and the pieces that I was trying to keep together would all fall out of place? I had to stay strong, I had to be whole for Skylar. Little did I know, she was what got me through that.

And she's going to be the one that gets me through this. I have to do this for her. I will save her, I don't know how, or if it's even possible, but I promised I'd protect her, and I won't let her down. If I lose her, I'll lose myself. I don't want a world without her, especially this insanely screwed-up world.

A warm touch startles me, and I'm surprised to see Quinn's hand on my elbow.

"You okay?" she asks.

"Yeah, sorry, I got lost in thought there for a moment."

"I understand, but try to stay with me here, don't leave me alone with this guy."

She lets out a small laugh, but I know she's more serious than she leads on.

Sanchez walks ahead, with nearly fifty feet between us. Changing courses slightly, he peers over his shoulder and motions with his rifle to follow him. Quinn and I pick up our pace and catch up to him.

"We're almost there, only a little farther." He motions again, this time up ahead.

The forest all appears the same, tree after tree after tree. Minimal paths mark the ground, random bushes and overgrown grass fill the voids. The ground is drying from all the rain we've had lately, although it's still on the softer side. I look ahead to where he motioned, and, in the distance, the fender of what I'm assuming is our vehicle pokes out.

I brace myself for what's to come and say a silent prayer that everything will be okay, that it will all go to plan.

We'll take the vehicle straight to town.

We'll go to the clinic.

We'll get the supplies.

We'll try to find a body along the way.

We'll stay alive.

There is a very real possibility that I could die today. And even though it would suck, it's something I find myself not totally terrified of. Don't get me wrong, death is a scary thing, the finality of it, but so is living. Living knowing all that has been lost, and suffering through a constant internal battle of never being able to change the past.

I would never be able to do it myself, but given the circumstance, if I had to die for the greater good, I would face it without fear. And there's a sort of calm in that, in accepting whatever life, or death, throws at you.

I know I'm expendable. No matter how Max tries to reassure me, it doesn't make it any less true. Keith is capable of doing everything I've done, and all I seem to be is an extra mouth to feed. I don't want to be a burden to them, but it's difficult to see it any other way.

Cynthia was my rock, securing me firmly with her kindness and assurances, helping me wade through the endless cycle of self-loathing. I was content, perhaps even happy, with her. It's not right to *need* someone so desperately, but we were opposites that attracted, and her absence is like losing this gigantic chunk of myself.

I get a glimpse of that same thing with Max, the way he looks at Skylar, the constant determination he has to stay by her side and begging her to return to him. I may not know their story, but I know enough to understand she means the world to him, and that if he lost her, it would open up an infinite void I'm all too familiar with.

Maybe that's why I'm drawn to help him, to help her. The world doesn't deserve to continue to lose great loves. Their family has already lost so much. Keith briefly but painfully told me about losing his wife, Max's mother, unexpectedly. The fleeting story paved the way to my understanding of Max's intense love, only being natural, considering his parents.

If I stay determined, focus on helping him save her from this consuming illness, use this as a distraction from the constant agony, perhaps there is hope for me. Cynthia would have wanted that. So I'll put on my happy face, wear this situation like a bandage over a seeping wound, and pray it gets me to the other side of this torment.

11

———

MAX

I shift uncomfortably in the rear seat of Sanchez's Toyota. Quinn called shotgun, totally catching me off guard. Half the time she doesn't say anything, and then sometimes she surprises me with her sense of humor. I can't help but think it's all part of some act, that she's desperately trying to hold her shit together. But then part of me thinks that maybe she's better at handling things than I am. Maybe I have something to learn from her.

She looks to me kindly and offers a smile. "You okay? You're not going to get car sick, are you?"

I shake my head. "No, I'm good."

Sanchez chimes in, "If you puke, you're cleaning it up."

"I'm not going to puke, guys. I'm fine."

"Do you know how to get to the clinic?" Sanchez asks.

"Yep, it's not far at all. I think we only live like ten...maybe fifteen minutes outside of town."

Quinn blurts, "Really? I thought we were farther out than that."

"I'm saying *town* very loosely. 'Town' is like a dollar general and a gas station. We happened to luck out and there's a small clinic. The guy who runs the place mostly does house calls for the elderly folk who still live around here and can't travel to the city."

We come to an intersection, not a car in sight. The orange glow of morning light bounces across the farm fields, corn already past the knee-high-by-fourth-of-July requirement. We sit there for a second, and I catch a glimpse of Sanchez wide-eyed in the rearview mirror, waiting on my direction.

"Oh, sorry, turn left. Then it's only up a way."

"Yes, sir," he replies—always so formal.

My mind wanders with purpose to whether or not we should be putting our trust in Sanchez. My gut tells me there's something he's simply not saying, something important. But I could be wrong. I was wrong about Quinn, I was wrong about my dad, I was wrong about Skylar. This thought of Skylar brings me back full force.

"Do you know what supplies you'll need?"

Quinn shifts in her seat to face me, her seat belt digging into her neck awkwardly. "Yeah, I have a general idea of what I need, what I'm hoping is there, and the bare necessities. You said this is a little doctor's office or something?"

"Yeah, it's a decently small office, but the guy treated nearly everything. I think he even performs minor surgeries, although I have no idea if it was up to code."

Quinn shakes her head. "We should be good then."

"I hate to be this guy right now, but do we have a plan for this whole getting a body for my dad thing?"

Sanchez, hands on the wheel, attention on the road, replies, "And I hate to admit this out loud, but I think we're going to have to wing it, improvise a bit."

"Sounds dangerous," Quinn adds.

"We'll figure it out, ma'am."

"You can just call me Quinn, no need for formalities."

"Thank you, ma'am—err, sorry, Quinn."

Approaching the town, Quinn and Sanchez exchange a smile. My gaze shifts anxiously across the tiny town, it's barren and desolate nature both welcoming and downright creepy. Adelphi isn't typically crowded by any means, but seeing it like this—empty—is unsettling.

Our SUV slows to a creep, and I point ahead. "The clinic is the last building on this block."

Sanchez rolls up to the building and puts the vehicle into park, cutting the ignition.

We let out a collective deep breath, and Quinn breaks the silence.

"It appears we're alone, that's a plus."

"I wouldn't be so naïve. Always assume the worst but hope for the best."

He's either a wise man, or a smart-ass—I'm still working on figuring out which.

"We move as a team. You follow my lead, my direction. Do as I say, and we get through this without issue."

Quinn nods and glances to me.

I nod in agreement. "Yes, sir."

"All right, then, let's go."

Once we've all exited the vehicle, we walk the few feet to the front door of the clinic. Quinn tries to peak inside, but the glass is that one-way type, where you can see out but you can't see in. So instead, she does a lousy job smashing her face to the front glass with no success. Sanchez wiggles the front door handle and confirms that it is locked.

He looks to me. "Keep an eye out, sir." And with one swift movement, he lifts his rifle and forces the butt of it into the door's window.

Glass shatters, and the large crashing sound has me certain that someone will hear, someone will come, and something bad is about to happen. But instead, we stand there in silence, letting the reverberations of what happened, happen. Nothing. No people, no bad things, only silence. A few seconds pass, what feels like forever, and a dog barks in the distance, startling us all.

I'm grateful it's merely a dog, but then I'm struck by the sad realization that there are probably animals, people's pets, all over the place that have no owners, no one to take care of them.

Quinn breaks the silence. "That's sad."

Sanchez, eyebrows furrowed in utter confusion, inquires, "Excuse me?"

"Oh, just, that dog. I hope he's okay and he's not starving to death or something."

He shakes his head. "I'm sure he will be fine. Now here, continue keeping an eye out."

He reaches his hand through the glass and opens the clinic's front door. The door leads into a small corridor, where another door is located to get into the clinic.

One by one, we step into the corridor, still no commotion from outside. We settle into the small space and a foul odor fills my lungs. Rotten eggs, it definitely smells of rotten eggs.

I quickly cover my face. "Do you smell that?"

Sanchez, clear as day and totally unfazed, declares, "Death."

"That's what I thought, I just didn't want to say it," Quinn states.

"Oh, god, it's gross."

"That's definitely something, or someone, decomposing. Yay med school."

Sanchez insists, "Do your best to take your t-shirts and cover your mouth and nose. It's only going to get worse inside, if that's where it's coming from." He pauses, allowing us to cover ourselves accordingly. "You ready?"

"Ready as I'll ever be."

He lets out a sigh, gives us a firm nod, and then breaks the glass of the remaining door with his rifle. "Let's go."

And just like that, we're through the threshold of the clinic and swimming in a thick fog of death.

12

MAX

I swallow the bile rising in my throat and press my t-shirt tighter around my nose and mouth. My eyes uncontrollably water, and I have to raise my right arm to wipe at them with my shirt sleeve. I scan the room, and it's exactly as I remember.

My childhood consisted of a few trips here. Stitches in my left eyebrow from running straight into a tree branch during an epic game of hide-and-seek, resetting my shoulder the time I fell off the porch, that gnarly chunk of glass I accidentally stepped on in the yard that I had to have removed.

"I don't think anyone is here," Quinn affirms, muffled under the minimal protection of her forest-green shirt. "Follow me over here. I'm assuming there are supplies this way."

"Yes, ma'am."

We make our way down the long narrow hallway, a few patient rooms on one side, offices on the other.

We reach the farthest room without issue, and I wonder if I worked myself up for no reason. Quinn stops in front of the door, which happens to be one of those half doors, I think it's called a Dutch door—my grandparents had one on their front porch, and they often left it open in the spring and fall, and those perfect summer evenings, filling their house with such sweet, fresh air.

As I look past the door and into the room, there is nothing but darkness. The light is off, and not much natural illumination fills this space of the clinic; I think that's typically preferred for these types of medical situations. Quinn places her hand gently on the door handle and looks from me to Sanchez.

Lifting his rifle and aiming into the dark room, he nods.

The breeze from the door being pushed open shoves a swift rotten-cabbage-like smell out and I fight the urge to vomit even more than earlier.

"What the...?"

Sanchez speaks, "Flip the light on, ma'am."

Quinn reaches into the room blindly, feeling around on the wall, frantically trying to find the light switch. It takes my eyes a moment to adjust, and when they do, I locate the cause of the horrid smell.

A man.

The man, actually.

The old guy, Dr. Lombardi, lying lifeless on the ground, slumped against the wall and the shelf. A syringe in one hand, a vial in the other. His body stiff, bloated, gray, and motionless.

Quinn takes a step forward, and Sanchez reaches an arm out to stop her.

"This is strange," she emphasizes.

"What is, ma'am?" Sanchez replies.

"He hasn't been dead long, a few days maybe."

"How do you know?"

"The rate in which his body is decomposing, it leads me to believe this is sort of recent." She kneels and tries to get a closer look at the vial in the man's hands. "This appears to be a multidose influenza vaccine." Continuing to cover her mouth and throat, she leans over the man. "He has multiple entry marks; I think he gave himself several doses."

Sanchez clears his throat, something he does often before speaking. "One of the ways this virus was being spread was through vaccines. The vaccine supplies were easily accessible, which made it a likely target, along with the public water supply."

Why does he know this?

"Ma'am, if you don't mind, can you verify the supplies you need are here?" He nods toward the huge medical supply area.

"Yes, of course, sorry," she agrees.

She seizes a box off the shelf, takes a small breath, and releases her shirt, freeing up her other hand to open the box, revealing face masks. She quickly puts one on and then hands one to me and Sanchez. "It's not much, but at least it will give us our hands and reduce the number of breathable bacteria."

"Thank you," I say once the mask is secure on my face, the stretchy ear loops pulling slightly on my overgrown hair.

Quinn snatches more things off the shelves, some things I recognize, some things I don't. Saline bags, plastic tubing, empty syringes. Her eyes focused, her finger trailing each shelf, grabbing items as she finds what she needs. Sanchez holds his backpack open for her to drop her findings inside.

She stops abruptly. "Oh god, where's the"—she cuts herself off—"oh, right there, good."

Sanchez asks, "Is there anything else you would find useful, foreseeing any issues in the future, unrelated or not?"

"Ahh, good idea." She allows her focus to return to the supplies. "Max, I need your backpack."

I wiggle it off my shoulder and open it for her to put things inside. She takes packs of medicine, first-aid supplies, and turns to us. "Is anyone diabetic?"

"Not that I'm aware of." I look to Sanchez and find him shrugging.

She studies multiple boxes of medicine, reading the contents, sometimes putting them in the backpack, sometimes returning them to the shelf.

"I just don't want to take something someone else might need, ya know? But want to make sure we have what we need." Her voice is slightly muffled under her mask.

"I understand, ma'am. I don't want to rush you, but if you think we have everything, we should be on our way."

It's then that I remember the rest of our plan—we need bodies.

"We have to bring a body, my dad needs samples."

"Ah, that reminds me." An imaginary lightbulb flickers over Quinn's head. "I'll grab some evacuated collection tubes."

"What?" It's like trying to understand someone who speaks a foreign language.

"Nothing, hang on." She takes more stuff off the shelf and shoves it into my bag. "All right, I'm good."

"This way, ma'am," Sanchez instructs, motioning toward the door and stepping out of the room first and making his way down the hallway.

As we're about to enter the waiting room, he stops dead in his tracks, which throws us all off balance.

From the rear, I ask, "What's wrong?"

He responds by taking a step in the area behind the front desk, allowing us to peer in around him and see the reason for his startling stop.

"We have another body," he declares.

Quinn, watching closely from her spot barely outside the front desk area, concludes, "Yeah, but I don't think this one is dead."

13

———

MAX

I lost the whole 'shotgun' thing—something I continue to suck at—so now I'm riding in the back with this half-alive woman we took from the clinic. To say I'm creeped out is an understatement. I mean, what the actual... Is this even safe?

We lowered the third-row seating, allowing room to put the woman in the very rear of the SUV. Lifting her body and placing it inside felt all sorts of wrong. The tension between the rest of us growing tremendously.

Quinn shifts in her seat to face me. "You all right?"

"Yeah, you don't think she'll wake up or anything, do you? I mean, how do we even know she's infected?"

"It's really the only explanation for her condition," she reassures. "I checked her vitals, I cracked the salts—if she was going to come to, it would have been then, not now."

My mind returns me to the lake, to the old, fragile woman lying on the floor in the bait shop, taking her last breath as I stepped over her and stole the keys to the boats. I thought it was my fault, I blamed myself. I somehow thought that my accidental touching her was what set her over the edge.

"Is she going to die?" I ask, partially meaning this woman, partially meaning Skylar.

She hesitates and then answers, almost analyzing the meaning behind my question, "I don't know. We should get her to Keith before we make any judgments."

Sanchez responds, not taking his eyes off of the road, "We should be there soon, ma'am."

Quinn adds, "If the woman and doctor were alive at the same time, before whatever happened, happened, she may not have been this way for long."

Our vehicle slows to a stop, distracting me from the woman positioned uncomfortably too close to me. "What's wrong?"

"Up ahead," Sanchez informs.

Through the windshield, I note the same thing we saw on the way here, the same corn, the same road, the same path we took not too long ago.

Except for one thing.

"Is that a truck up ahead?"

"Yes, sir."

"That definitely wasn't there on the way in. Are we on the same road?" The roads out here all look the same, farm fields lining both sides of the street.

"Yes, sir. I went the same way we came."

"What are we going to do?" Quinn asks.

"Ma'am, I think we should continue ahead, but cautiously."

"Why is it just sitting there, on the road?" I squint, trying to confirm whether or not the truck is moving.

"Maybe it broke down," Quinn proposes.

I glance in the trunk of our SUV. So far, no visible changes; the woman hasn't mysteriously come back to life and attacked me or anything. She simply lies there, fairly motionless, less the small amount of shallow, sporadic breathing. She almost looks peaceful, as if she's purely taking a nap—a death nap.

We make our way toward the truck, which, the closer we get, appears to be blocking the majority of the road, parked sideways, right in the middle. Its stupid extended cab and over-sized tires take up entirely too much room. The black paint and bright-orange flames remind me of those guys who try way too hard to be cool but end up looking like idiots instead. The guys who think getting wasted every chance they get is what turns girls on, and who can't keep a girl because they can't seem to stay loyal due to their overinflated ego, thinking they deserve multiple girls at one time. And to top it off, the overindulgence of Axe body spray and chewing tobacco—yeah, that's the kind of guy who drives this kind of truck.

Quinn breaks the silence. "What kind of douche would drive this?"

"My thoughts exactly," I laugh.

"The passenger door appears to be open, which is sort of strange," Sanchez notes. "I'm going to go around it on the right side. I haven't seen any people. Maybe they broke down and took off on foot."

"But why are they parked sideways?" Quinn asks.

"There is a very real possibility that this is a trap, that's why. I'm hoping I'm wrong, but this feels like a trap," Sanchez concludes.

Quinn, open-mouthed in a panic, shrieks, "What—why would you drive us into a trap?"

"Sorry, ma'am. I ran a risk assessment and I feel confident we will be fine."

"Please, *stop* calling me ma'am!" Still startled, she asks, "What do you mean, 'risk assessment'?"

"It's what I do. I assess the situation to determine the prob-able outcomes, risks, and alternatives. I feel comfortable, given our resources and situation, we will be fine."

Quinn glances hopefully to me as if to back her up, but I

shrug. I desperately want to be home. I may not trust that Sanchez is telling us the whole truth, but I trust that he will get us out of whatever this is.

We make our way off the road slightly, approaching the bed of the deserted truck, all of our attention shifting from one thing to another, and I frantically hope this isn't a trap.

I let out a breath, realizing that I was holding it, as we get all four tires securely on the pavement.

"Well, that wasn't so bad, was it?" I say.

Quinn gives me a death stare and then lightens up. "I guess not."

We pick up our pace along this back-country road, and I worry that we should have stopped to confirm if we could have offered our help. Maybe the people ran out of gas or got a flat tire—I didn't even think to check for the cause of why they were stopped, although we didn't see any people, not around the truck and not on the way toward it.

Then it hits me. Maybe they walked this direction.

"Should we keep an eye out for those people or something? I didn't see anyone on the way there, or at the truck."

"Don't be foolish, sir, we have more pressing issues to focus on."

He's right, I can't play hero all the time, I can't save everyone. Maybe that's my problem, I try to help too many people and inadvertently help no one.

Right at that thought, something flashes across my peripheral. It takes a moment to register it's a vehicle.

"What the hell?" I say, turning around in my seat to see behind us.

Sanchez stomps the accelerator. "Buckle up."

The vehicle—a small, red Honda-something—fishtails before regaining itself, and then catapults the distance between us, bumping violently into our SUV. I glance down to the woman in the back of our vehicle, still unfazed by the current events, and then to the car driving erratically behind us. The driver, a middle-aged bald man, white-knuckling the steering wheel while doing his best to stay close behind us. The passenger, another middle-aged man, smoking a cigarette and yelling at his driver, what I'm assuming is to keep on our tail.

"This is bad, this is really bad," I say to whoever is listening.

"I thought this might happen," Sanchez announces.

I find myself unsure of how to react to his semi-emotionless declaration.

14

———

QUINN

"Shit, shit shit," Max mutters from the back seat.

Sanchez, seemingly unaffected, continues driving, pushing the accelerator steadily, his amber-colored hands firmly gripping the steering wheel. I study his face for any type of reaction, his dark eyebrows, slightly furrowed but otherwise impassive. His deep eyes, soft but fearless, dart to the rearview mirror and then return to the desolate road ahead.

I shift in the passenger seat, straining to look through the rear glass at the small car tailing us closely. The car darts from right to left erratically.

"Can you lose them?" I ask.

"That is the plan, ma'am."

I cringe. I don't know why exactly it bothers me that he calls me ma'am, but although I've asked him a million times to stop, he keeps insisting. Maybe because it makes me feel old. And maybe because it's weirdly unsettling that he remains heavily formal, leaving me to wonder if he's hiding something. I know Max thinks he is, I see the way he studies Sanchez any time he speaks—he does it so obviously. But, I really can't blame him. This guy manages to show up, wielding all this knowledge, single-handedly brings home someone they thought might have been dead, and is, obviously, military-trained. I think we've all been studying Sanchez, trying to figure out his secrets.

My thoughts are interrupted when Sanchez urges, "Hold on," while almost simultaneously stomping on the brakes.

My seat belt locks, throwing my body forward, and I somehow know I'm going to have a bruise from the impact. Tires screech, and the idiots behind us miraculously maneuver scarcely quick enough to avoid slamming into us. I can only imagine how bad that would have been if they would have actually hit us.

"What the hell, man?" Max shouts, clearly unhappy about Sanchez's decision.

"It was expected, sir. I said to hold on," Sanchez commands, still maintaining eye contact on the rearview mirror. Without looking, he reaches forward and flips a switch. A sequence of sounds and metal clanking follows, and then something seems to lock in place.

"What if they would have hit us? I'd be dead!"

I interrupt his angry rant. "Is the woman okay?"

He seems to shake his head and sighs, turning to glance into the back of the SUV. "Yeah, she's just all crumpled, and seems super uncomfortable." He pauses for a moment, studying her. "She's still breathing."

"Good," I say, temporarily relieved she isn't dead yet.

Max's voice slightly elevated. "What are we waiting for, Sanchez?"

"Their move," Sanchez sneers, his eyes wild and yet somehow eerily calm.

"What?" we both say.

The men, parked not even a car length behind us on the passenger side, appear to be having a heated discussion. The passenger waves his gun and points to it with his other hand, and the driver shakes his head and mouths something. Finally, the driver shoves the passenger hard in the shoulder and hisses loud enough for us to hear, "You do it!"

At that cue, the passenger huffs, muffles something to the driver, and stomps out of the car.

"Dude!" Max hollers. "Dude, they're coming, get us out of here!"

But Sanchez doesn't move, doesn't really do anything other than keep his eyes on the rearview mirror.

I swallow the lump forming in my throat and decide to put my blind faith in whatever plan Sanchez has formed, but not told us.

As the passenger—a disgusting-looking man, belly protruding and snot-nose—places both feet onto the pavement, Sanchez says quietly, almost to himself, "There we go."

Before Max or I can even ask what he meant, he pushes onto the accelerator, lurching us forward. The gross man shoots his gun, poorly, in our direction before barreling like an idiot into his vehicle, clearly pissed off. In a matter of seconds, we're easing off the road, heading straight into a field full of corn.

The men, following closely, have a harder time maneuvering over the small ditch on the side of the road. Their car's low-profile front end hits the embankment and splinters their bumper, lodging it under the driver's side tire. I become thankful for the higher clearance of our SUV, watching intently as it plows through layers of corn the height of mailboxes. We turn right, into the corn, and continue to make our way farther into the field.

As each moment passes, we get a little farther from the car. Right when I feel like we might actually get away, I'm jolted in my seat by an abrupt stop, followed by the thrusting motions that the SUV is making.

"Only a minor disturbance," Sanchez cuts himself off right as he was about to say 'ma'am'. Maybe all the dirty looks paid off.

Sanchez rocks the SUV back and forth for a few moments, trying to ease us out of the hole. Max and I turn our attention to the car closing in behind us, now missing the front bumper. The car picks up speed and unnaturally jerks from front to back as it hits minor bumps in the terrain. Barreling toward us, they don't let up, and just when I'm certain we're about to get smashed from behind, our SUV somehow lurches out of the hole and shoots forward, freeing us from impending doom.

"Step on it," Max asserts from the back seat, eyes still fixated on the car behind us.

The car takes the identical path toward us and slams violently into the same hole we were stuck in. The passenger tire somehow dislodges and projectiles itself simultaneously as the passenger, who isn't buckled up, smashes into the dashboard. We watch, fixated on the vehicle and men becoming smaller the farther away we get. Sanchez remains steady on the accelerator, pushing us through the field, continuing to pummel the premature corn stalks.

"I think they're stuck for good," I say.

Sanchez shifts his eyes to the rearview and nods in agreement.

"A little heads-up would be nice," Max deadpans.

"I could not be certain, so I did not say anything, sir."

"You could have said *something*," Max reiterates. "You're going to get us killed. We're a team now, and the whole team needs to know what's going on."

Surprisingly, Sanchez replies, "You're right."

By this, Max seems unsure what to say next.

"The lady still all right?" I ask.

"Yeah, for now."

It's utterly insane that we have an unconscious woman in the vehicle. An *infected* unconscious woman. She could turn on us at any moment and either become deranged or simply die. I can't imagine she'll easily snap out of whatever comatose state she's in and be like "Hey guys, who are you? Where are we going? What's for lunch?" My fingers are crossed that she will pose to be some kind of help for figuring out what's going on with Skylar and what is happening to the world around us. Keith is a smart man, and I believe he will be able to figure *something* out. He has to—the whole world is counting on it, at least that's what I've gathered from overhearing his conversations with Sanchez.

We head toward the street in the distance, the sound of our breathing and the crunch of the corn stalks filling the space. We cross the ditch with ease and enter the road, only to come to a brief stop. Sanchez flips a switch, and the familiar metal clanks again.

I raise my eyebrow in his direction.

"Four-wheel drive," he elaborates.

"Ohhh."

We start driving once more, and Sanchez notifies, "We're going to have to take an alternate route."

"Why," Max questions.

Sanchez's eyes shift to the rearview. "We're leaving a trail."

I look in the side mirror to see the mud path our SUV is leaving in the road.

"Crap," I say quietly.

"I can't imagine they'll find it any time soon, being stuck in the field and all, but if they were with others, or there are others, I don't want it to lead them straight to the cabin," Sanchez says.

"So, what's the plan?" Max probes, rubbing his chin.

"Do you have any ideas?" Sanchez asks, clearly doing his best to be a part of a team. He adjusts the rearview and watches Max, waiting for a response.

15

——

MAX

I'm caught off guard by his response, and it takes me a minute to let my mind process the information. This is progress, this is good. He's being inclusive instead of exclusive. I can work with this. Quinn stares at me, and for a second I think I feel the heat from her glare, waiting for me to speak, to say anything.

I quickly scan the road ahead, trying to figure out where we are.

"Up there, not too far up ahead." I point. "There's an old farmhouse. We could spray the mud off and be on the road in no time."

"And how will we spray the mud off?" Quinn asks.

"Oh, right, yeah, there's probably a water pump. It's fairly common around here. And like I said, the farmhouse is old, like abandoned old. With all the rain we've had, I'm sure we'll be good."

"Farmhouse it is," Sanchez speaks. "That giant brick one on the left?"

"Yes, sir."

"Funny," he teases.

I shrug then shift my focus to the back of the SUV, to the woman, still lying there partially lifeless. From the ride, she managed to somehow untangle her body from the crumpled-up mess I saw her in from the excursion through the field. I can only imagine the aches and pains she'll feel if she wakes up, being thrown around like that—it's a surprise she didn't break her neck. We should have been more cautious with how she was secured, but it's not like we could have anticipated a pursuit like that.

My mind wiggles its way free of this woman and lingers on Skylar, something I find myself uncontrollably (and controllably) doing, nearly all the time. It's rare if, at any given moment, my mind isn't thinking about her in some capacity.

The woman reminding me of Skylar.

Wanting Skylar to be okay, *needing* Skylar to be okay.

Imagining Skylar being okay and simply being able to talk to her, to hear her voice.

To tell her that everything is going to be okay and hear her tell me the same.

I let her down, I broke my promise. I was supposed to keep her safe, to protect her. When I failed her, I failed myself.

I permit my thoughts to return to her journal, to the few entries I allowed myself the pleasure of indulging. The one where she talked about the pain of not having anyone to rely on, how everyone has let her down in some capacity. How she felt responsible for having expectations of people, how she doesn't feel as though she expects much, just common decency, but she fails to receive that. How her mom flakes on her over and over, how she wished she had a mom who was more involved, who cared enough about their daughter to be there during the times she was needed most. How her dad promised he'd quit drinking, but what that meant was that he would quit drinking liquor, and still gets drunk every day. How nearly every guy she's considered showing interest in ends up sleeping with her friends or turning out to be a creep. How she desperately wants one good thing in her life. How she doesn't think she'll ever really be happy because she feels like she expects so little and gets even less.

My heart broke reading her words. I don't think I've ever related more, but in my own unique way. Life feels like this constant battle of not knowing who anyone really is, expecting the best and getting the worst. Assuming people are genuine and mean well, when most people are selfish and only have themselves in mind. Don't get me wrong, there are good people out there, but they are so heavily covered and concealed by all the bad, it's hard to find them. And it's especially harder when you're shielding yourself and putting up your own walls and guards, so the bad ones don't break through and take advantage.

It reminds me of this story I read once about this person who put on a mask every day to hide their true identity but tried so desperately to find someone like them, so they could take their mask off and be free. The other person was also wearing a mask, so every day they walked past each other without knowing, and it wasn't until one person finally decided to be themselves, that the other person finally found them.

This is me taking my mask off. I know I won't be perfect and I'll make mistakes, but I know I can be a good person, that I am a good person, and I can be the one thing that Skylar can finally count on. And I won't give up trying to be a better version of myself and helping her be a better version of herself. She deserves that, I deserve that.

My heart aches at the impossibility of the situation. I might not ever get the chance to say any of this to her, to let her know of our potential. The unknown weighs on me heavily, like a thick cloak that cannot be removed, and the likelihood that she very well could be dead when I return to her breaks my heart in two.

Our tires touch gravel, and the sound, along with the slight bumbling of the shift in terrain, brings me viciously to this reality. The reality of so many unknowns all around us. I quickly scan what I can see of the property.

"You okay?" Quinn asks, her contemplative eyes peering into my soul.

I muster a fake smile and say, "Yeah," although I know she knows, she knows more than she lets on. I'm terrible at hiding my emotions at times, and Quinn knows all too well what I'm going through, so she sees straight through my shoddy attempts to conceal them.

Sanchez eyes something in the distance. "You were right, Max. There's a water pump up ahead." He nods toward the pump, on the far side of the house.

Relief floods through me. I didn't know for sure if there would be one here, I just didn't want to not have a possible solution when he asked me earlier.

"Let's park, assess the situation," Sanchez says.

"Good deal."

Quinn points a few feet away from the pump. "There's a hose under that picnic table."

The SUV comes to a slow stop, and Sanchez puts it in park. We all let out a collective sigh and turn toward each other in a slight huddle. Teamwork!

Sanchez communicates first. "I haven't seen anyone, and we should be shielded behind the house and not visible from the road."

"Two people clean us off, one stay behind? What do you guys think?" I offer.

Our eyes shift back and forth to each other.

Sanchez orders, "Quinn stays, in the driver's seat, keeping an eye out for us, and on the lady in case she comes to."

"Okay," she confirms.

"Then, let's do this," Sanchez directs, authority seeping from his pores, something that must come naturally to him.

Within a minute, I've gathered and attached the hose to the pump while Sanchez maintains a lookout. Still no sign of life, or death. The wind picks up for a brief second, and the warm breeze grounds me to this summer day. We make quick progress on ridding the SUV of its mud, making sure to hose the old brick driveway, too. I ask Quinn to pull up a little bit, so I can get the whole tire, and in a matter of seconds, we're done. It's that simple.

Sanchez and I hop into the SUV and Quinn settles comfortably into the passenger seat. I wipe my hands on my jeans and relax into the seat, only then re-remembering the woman lodged in here with me. A chill runs through me. Life is weird.

I reach across and buckle my seat belt, securing my place behind Sanchez.

"We ready?" he asks.

"Let's go home," I say.

And just like that, we're turning around in the big driveway behind the house and starting our journey around the rear side of the house, toward the street. Right as we pick up a little speed, I'm startled by a blur that darts across my vision, heading toward us. Sanchez does his best to slam on the brakes, but before we can stop, we've hit whatever ran across our path.

"What was that?" I ask, unbuckling my seat belt and leaning forward.

Quinn turns to me, her golden eyes bulging, stammering with a shaky voice, "A person."

16

———

MAX

"What do you mean *a person?*" I ask, heart accelerating fiercely.

Quinn begins to speak, but Sanchez cuts her off.

"Stay put, I'll be right back." Without allowing us to interject, he jumps out of the vehicle, gun drawn.

My mind starts going wild—did we accidentally kill someone? Sanchez disappears under the hood of our SUV momentarily, and immediately as panic boils inside me, he stands up and motions for us to come.

I take a quick peek into the trunk before exiting the vehicle, the woman still alive and unconscious. I step onto the driveway, close the door, and immediately I see feet sticking out, attached to legs, attached to a man. A man who we just ran over.

My hand instinctually goes to cover my mouth. "Is he dead?"

Quinn, kneeling next to the man, her fingers resting under his chin, placed gently against his neck, speaks quietly, "No."

"Can I be honest?" Sanchez asks. Before we can answer, he adds, "I think he's deranged."

"What, how?" I say.

At this, Quinn stands, turns her attention to Sanchez, the doctor in her coming to life. "What makes you say that?" she asks.

Sanchez studies the man for a moment, while we wait eagerly for him to respond. "I saw his face."

"Yes, and what about his face?" she says.

"He looked pissed."

"He could have needed help or thought we were robbing the property," she offers. "Or he could have been with that group of people."

"Speaking of, we should probably get a move on it," I suggest.

Ignoring me, Sanchez says, "It was his eyes, they were swollen, bright red. His fists were balled up like he wanted to hit something." He glances from the man to Quinn, "I've seen enough of them, and the more that I think about it, he was definitely deranged."

"Okay," is all that Quinn says, walking to the SUV, opening the rear door and fumbling with something inside.

She returns with a syringe in her hand, holds it out for us to see, and then kneels carefully down and injects it into the man's arm, doing her best to be precise. Luckily, the man's veins are bulging, so she finds her target easily.

"This should kick in fairly soon, if not within the minute. I'm unsure how long it will last, based on the dosage, so we need to move fast."

Quinn stares from me to Sanchez, as if expecting a specific response.

"Because we're taking him with us..." she replies slowly to make sure we understand.

"Ohh, right," I say, feeling like an idiot. I guess we did come out here for bodies.

"You grab his feet, I'll grab his torso," Sanchez commands.

I wrap my hands around his ankles and motion to the SUV. "Can you open the hatch and reposition that lady? Make room for this guy."

"Yes, of course."

"Grab him under his knees," Sanchez demands.

"You said his feet," I correct.

"Have you never..." he mutters and shakes his head. "Never mind, grab him under his knees. It'll be easier to hold him. Lift with your legs, not your back."

I do what he says, and we're able to carry the man around to the opening of the SUV with relative ease.

We approach, and Quinn has rearranged the woman and is hopping out of the trunk area.

"I had to put one of the seats down to make room. I'm thinking you can lay him sideways in there." She motions toward the available space.

The woman is partially in the back seat and partially in the trunk area.

"Oh, and I still call shotgun," Quinn adds.

Great, this unconscious woman is going to be *right* next to me. It was one thing when she was in the very back, with the seat as a somewhat barricade, but now she's pretty much my seat partner. At least it's not the man. If I had to choose a comatose or a deranged, I guess I would choose the former. I don't think she will come to life and beat me to death. But, anything is possible in this world.

"Thanks," I say, heavily laced with sarcasm.

Sanchez hoists his end of the man into the SUV, and I help him arrange the rest of the body. Sanchez pushes the electronic hatch closure, and just like that, we have kidnapped two people. I didn't realize it would be this simple. I shouldn't get ahead of myself, though, we still have the rest of the trip home.

And the chances of this lady dying, or the man coming to and killing us are pretty high. I forgot to mention the men we left stranded in the cornfield; they're probably coming after us right this moment. The likelihood of us getting home safely is decreasing by the minute.

"We should hurry," I advise.

Sanchez nods, and we all return into our respective seating arrangement.

"How effective is that sedative?" I ask Quinn.

I don't want to buckle, because I don't want to be stuck in place and not able to see what's going on around me, but I decide it's the best option. I do my best to sit at an angle, back pressed slightly against the door to give me a better view of the people hanging out in here with me.

"I'd say it's fairly effective, accompanied by the blow to the head rendering him unconscious. We should be okay."

"And *okay* is good, right?"

She lets out a small chuckle. "Yes, Max, *okay* is good, you can relax."

"I'd like to see you relax, being stuck so close to *them*." I motion to our passengers.

She shrugs. "You could have called shotgun."

"Yeah, yeah," I mumble, looking out the window as we drive slowly onto the road. The slight shift in pavement startles me, and I nearly jump out of my seat to make sure these people haven't woken up.

I shake my head, trying to rid myself of my nerves. It feels like it's one thing after another. When will the chaos stop? I'm fairly certain I'm going to end up having a heart attack soon from the constant adrenaline coursing through me. I take a deep breath, in through my nose deeply and out my mouth.

I close my eyes, and Skylar comes to the forefront immediately. My hand on her back, helping her sit on the steps at our house, only a mere couple weeks ago.

"Anxiety," she had said.

I couldn't begin to understand then, the trauma she's experienced from her past. Reflecting on it now, it makes sense why she was so distant and would only give herself in pieces at a time. It was almost like she subconsciously felt comfortable enough to open up, and then at the slightest thing, she returned to reality and shut herself down. I don't blame her—I did something very similar to her. We all have our secrets, our demons that eat at us from the inside that no one can see. Every person has their own struggles.

I want so badly to fix this, to bring Skylar out and away from this mess. I would change places with her in a heartbeat if I could. I want her to know that I see her, that she can take her mask off. I don't expect anything from her, and if being her friend is all she wants, then I will be the best friend to her. Even if she wants nothing to do with me, I need her to know that I'm sorry, for all the things I've done, and for all the things the universe has put her through. Whatever version of me she needs, or wants, I'll be that for her.

Quinn shuffles in her seat and speaks low. "You all right?"

"Yeah, why, what's up?" I crinkle my nose and sniffle slightly.

"We're almost there, we're almost home."

My eyes shift from the unconscious passengers to the landscape around us. Bright-green foliage overflowing along a dirt road, leading us toward the cabin.

"How did you know how to get to the cabin?" I ask Sanchez.

"I just paid attention." His response unsettles me a little and I wonder what else he may have noticed or picked up on.

A thought strikes me. "Wait, are we parking where you were parked before?"

"Yes, why?" he queries, breaking his concentration only slightly to glance at me.

Quinn looks to me, too.

"How are they getting there?" I motion at our passengers.

"We'll have to carry them."

Greatttt. This should be fun.

17

MAX

After we park, we sit and brainstorm for a minute.

Sanchez, rubbing his chin, says, "I can carry the man. You two can carry the woman."

"How are you going to carry the guy, he's like, *really* big?" Quinn says.

"It makes the most sense, and I think it's the quickest option."

I shrug. "We could carry him, you could carry the lady. That would probably be the quickest option."

"You two would be slow with the man. I've had to carry men this size or maybe even larger in the past. I can handle it," he insists.

"Whatever we do, we really should hurry. I don't know how long that sedative will last," Quinn says.

"That's what I was thinking," Sanchez agrees.

"Okay," I say, conceding and going along with the plan, mainly because I desperately want to get back and see how everyone (Skylar) is doing. Now that the heavy guilt of Wiley's unknown whereabouts has lifted, Skylar is all I can think about;

it's all-consuming. It's probably not healthy, and it's probably borderline insanity, but I have no control over the way I feel about her.

We all throw our backpacks on and make our way to the rear of the SUV. Sanchez quickly, and with more ease than I expected, throws the deranged man over his shoulder. Sanchez grunts as he bends his knees and hoists the man into position, his arms dangling down Sanchez's backside. Quinn and I both grab an ankle and pull the woman to the end of the trunk area.

"Grab under her knees and walk that way," I say.

She follows my order, and I'm able to grip under the woman's torso just at the right time, the weight of her body falling into our arms.

Sanchez reaches over and pushes the button to lower the trunk lid and then fumbles in his pocket for a second, a chirp-chirp announcing the vehicle's locked position.

"This way," he commands with a nod.

Without a word, we follow.

I realize I've made a mistake with how I'm holding the woman, so I say, "Hold on a second," as I reposition her to be behind me. Now I can actually move forward and see where I'm going.

We walk in silence for a small eternity, my mind focusing on the small sounds around us. Birds chirping to each other, insects buzzing, our feet breaking the occasional twig, our labored breaths with each step toward the cabin. Thanks to the cover of the trees, we're not in direct sunlight, but it's still warm, and it's not long before a bead of sweat runs down my brow. My hands cramp, and I remind myself that we will be there soon.

Quinn breaks the quietness. "Sanchez?"

"You can call me Alex if you'd like."

"Oh," she says, slightly startled. "Okay, Alex. I have a question."

"And I have an answer," he says sarcastically, but in good humor.

She hesitates and then responds, "Are you...alone? I mean, do you have any family?"

Alex doesn't speak but lets out a long sigh, clearly harboring something he doesn't want to elaborate on. He walks a few steps ahead of us, allowing me to see the tension rising in his body, claiming a home in his shoulders and jaw.

"I had a family," is all he says.

Quinn softly says, "Me, too," and then the sounds of the forest around us become the only thing I hear.

We go the rest of the way in silence, a heavy sadness filling the space. Once we're in eyesight distance of the cabin, my dad breaks out in a sprint across what's left of the gap between us. My heart nearly falls apart. I can't bear the thought of something worse happening to Skylar. He can't be bringing me bad news. I won't accept it. Rushing forward with the woman between us, I urge my legs to move faster, Quinn struggling to keep up. My heart, beating so loud the sound fills my ears, almost blocking out Quinn telling me to slow down.

My dad places his hands on my shoulders, and tears fight to fill my eyes. We come to an abrupt stop, and I'm choking on my inability to speak. His eyes, panicked and red-rimmed, scan me from head to toe.

Visibly shaken, he asks, "Are you, are you all all right?"

"Just tell me please," I manage to get out, ignoring his question.

"Tell you w—?" he tries to say.

I cut him off. "Skylar, what happ—is she, god, is she okay?"

His hands still on my shoulders, he shakes his head. "Yes, yes, Max, Skylar is fine."

I nearly fall to my knees. It's everything I can do to stay put together, to not drop this woman and run straight to Skylar's side. I've never felt weaker in my life, hanging on the thread of what life Skylar has left.

"Why did you run? What's wrong?" I ask.

"When you have kids, you'll understand." He shifts his focus from me to Quinn. "You all right over there?"

The weight of the woman presses firmer in my grasp as Quinn shifts slightly and mutters, "Mmhmm."

"Here, let me." He reaches forward and takes the woman from Quinn. "What have we here?"

Quinn shifts into doctor-mode. "Woman, middle-aged. She shows signs of being comatose." She points to Sanchez. "Alex is carrying a man showing signs of being deranged. Both vitals seem stable at this point. The man has been sedated; I can show you the vial and dosage when we get inside. I'm unsure how long it will last."

"Intravenous or intramuscular?"

"Intravenous," she replies.

His eyes go wide. "How is that even...?" He shakes his head and continues, "Never mind, good job."

"Thank you," she says shyly.

"And the supplies?"

"Yes, we got what we needed, plus some."

"Good, good," he nods. "Okay, gang, let's get inside."

The urge to take off in a sprint to Skylar bubbles up, and I fight it with all my might. I remind myself I'm almost there, only a few more steps until I'm in the house, until I can see her, and see that she's okay. Only a little bit farther until we can get her the supplies she needs, to bring her back to me, or at least help her hold on longer until Dad and Quinn figure out how to save her.

18

————

MAX

Once I've entered the threshold of the cabin, I set the woman gently, but quickly, on the floor. I leave the group behind and take off in a sprint to my bedroom, my stomach seeming to rise into my throat and my heart pounding, somehow faster and slower at the same time. I burst through my bedroom door and then stop completely, moving cautiously the rest of the distance to her. My gaze stuck like glue to her, searches her over for the slightest change, the smallest sign of progress or deterioration.

Her hair is tucked ever so slightly behind her ears, the ends tangled together, in need of being brushed, and I make a mental note to do this later. The remnants of bruising on her cheek, the faintest reminder of the last few weeks events, is almost completely gone. My hand finds its place in hers, the chill of her skin seeping into mine, like fog making its way across a sleepy town.

"Oh god," I whisper as I sit on the bed, "I was so worried." I'm far past the point of feeling stupid for talking to an unconscious person. "We did it," I manage, forcing a bit of a smile. "We got supplies and we got two bodies. We ran into a bit of trouble, but we did it, Skylar." I pause in my speech and study the way her chin slopes at just the right angle. My gaze trails her nose, rounded in the most adorable way with what appears to be a small pin-point hole right on the crease of her left nostril, almost unnoticeable if you're not paying close attention. Did she have her nose pierced? "Please, come back." I bring her hand upward, press it against my lips. "Please," I beg.

Quinn appears behind me. "Do you want to help me, or do you want to go with the guys?"

"I'll stay," I murmur.

"Don't be squeamish, okay? If you pass out on the floor, I'm leaving you until I'm done."

"That seems fair."

She carries her bag into the room and places it next to Skylar, on the opposite side of her from me. She rummages through the contents, pulling things out and putting them on the bed. She stops for a second and glances up at me. "Go wash your hands." She looks almost apologetic.

"Oh, duh, of course. Be right back," I say, making my way out of the room.

I turn down the hallway and get to the bathroom at a brisk pace, tunnel vision the whole time. I place my hand on the doorknob and am startled when it turns, followed by Wiley emerging.

"Whoa! Hey, buddy!"

"Hey, I just need to wash my hands."

"Have you seen your dad?" Always with him trying to find my dad, what the heck.

But then that reminds me, I really have no idea what any of them have been doing since we returned from our supply trip. And I have no clue where they put the bodies.

I shake my head. "No. What are you guys doing?"

"He asked us to move the bodies but then he took off after

he grabbed samples. He did it so fast. Did you know your dad could do that?" His wide eyes are staring, waiting for a response.

I shake my head again, making sure to massage the soap between all of my fingers.

"That guy is crazy, your dad. He's so smart, we're lucky to have him."

"Listen, Wiley, I haven't seen him. Have you checked his office or the cellar?"

"We put the bodies in the cellar, so he must be in his office. You're so smart, you must get it from him."

"Thanks, I really need to get going, Quinn needs my help."

"Oh, right, yeah. Such a shame..." His face goes blank for a moment. "But we're lucky to have her."

"I don't disagree, but really, I have to get back."

I push past him, careful not to touch him with my clean hands. I'm about to enter my bedroom but stop short to glance down the hall. Wiley is blankly standing there, one hand on his hip and another scratching his head.

I holler down the hallway at him, "His office."

And at that, he snaps his fingers and points to me with a smile. I don't continue watching but can hear him make his way down the hallway and up the stairs.

When I enter my bedroom, Quinn doesn't even acknowledge me.

"What can I do," I say, making my way to the bedside. My gaze falls on Skylar, a thin tube coming from her nose taped to the side of her cheek.

Quinn fastens the length of the tube to Skylar's shirt with the clothespin.

"Wait, are you done?" And then it hits me. "You tricked me." A silent rage builds within. "Why would you do that?"

Quinn continues to attach miscellaneous items to the tubes, one of them a bag that I assume is a food source.

"I'm sorry, I really did need you to wash your hands, so I began without you." She shrugs. "When I realized I could use it as an opportunity to get it placed before you came back, I didn't hesitate. Whether you want to admit it or not, you are a bit squeamish. And without your dad here to keep you under control, it made sense. I've done this procedure numerous times, it's fairly easy. Conscious patients can even do it themselves, it's that simple."

"Oh," I say, and even though it makes sense, I still wish she would have waited for me.

"This isn't a long-term solution," she discloses.

I can't help but stare at her, pleading for the answers she isn't capable of giving me.

"Meaning, we can't keep it in forever. But it should give her the nutrients she needs in the short term until we figure out the next step."

"Thank you," I say in an unfamiliar voice—so small, almost a whisper.

She removes a glove from one hand and then takes that glove to remove the other, in a motion so smooth it wraps the other glove inside it for disposal. She places a hand on my shoulder, and I instinctually flinch.

"We're trying, okay?"

"I know, I just wish there was something else that could be done." Something like me being able to take her place.

"We'll figure it out," she says with a reassuring smile. "You really don't give your dad enough credit."

And at that cue, he pops his head around the door. "Hey, both of you." He points from Quinn to me. "I need blood samples."

"Did Wiley find you?" I ask.

"Yes," he says, slightly out of breath, "I had them take the bodies to the cellar, figured the minimal lighting and low temperature would keep them slightly dormant. But I need the samples, come on."

"What's wrong?" I ask, my concern rising as a result of his tone and pushiness.

"Nothing, I just have a hunch."

I glance over my shoulder at Skylar. "But..."

"She'll be okay for a few minutes, this won't take long, come on."

19

———

MAX

I know I should look away while he inserts the needle into my vein, but the repulsion and fascination both battle each other, leaving me unable to do anything but stare. A small prick of the needle sends a chill over me, and I find myself fixated on the small tube attached to gather the blood.

"You okay?" he asks.

I glance up, partially dazed and lightheaded but manage, "Yeah, I'm good."

"I forgot you were weird about needles."

I quickly change the subject. "What's the hunch?"

"What? Oh, it's only a theory I have," he answers, without giving me any more information. He flicks the tube slightly.

"So...what's the theory?"

"I'd rather see if I'm right first. I've had a dozen different theories so far, but this is the first solid lead."

He places a cotton ball where the needle is inserted and pulls the needle out, pressing the cotton ball into my arm. "That's it, just apply pressure." He reaches behind him, and when Quinn hands him a roll of medical tape, they exchange a minute smile.

"That was easy," I say, partially lying as I feel the wooziness not wanting to dissipate.

"You look rough, Max," Quinn says.

"I think my blood sugar is low or something," I say, which at first was purely a cover-up but could actually be the truth.

"Go grab something from the kitchen," Dad demands without fully taking his eye off the task at hand. He removes his gloves the same way Quinn did and puts on another pair. "You're next," he says to her.

She gives him her arm, and he immediately places a tourniquet around her biceps and wipes the spot with an alcohol pad. Not allowing any more time to be grossed out, I quickly make my way out of the room and to the kitchen. I briefly scan my options and settle on a fruit cup from the fridge, the same kind my mom packed in my lunch when I was a child. I open the cup of mixed fruit over the sink, because wow, they pack these things so full of juice it's almost impossible to open without making a mess, and down the contents quickly. I figure if the way I'm feeling is because of sugar, this should kick into my system pretty soon.

"All that sugar is bad for you," a person calls from behind me.

I turn to see Sanchez standing in the living room, leaned up against the doorframe.

"I thought I was going to pass out," I say.

He lets out a little chuckle. "You got your blood drawn."

"Yeah, I can't stand needles." I throw my trash into the garbage can in the closet.

He walks to the refrigerator and grabs a fruit cup, opening the top slightly and drinking some of the juice and then pulling the rest of the top off.

"What happened to *sugar being bad for you?*" I ask.

"Hey, we all have to indulge every now and then," he replies, toasting his fruit cup into the air and then consuming the innards. "These things are good." He smiles and wipes his mouth with his sleeve.

I hold my hand out for the trash. "Yeah, you're not wrong."

"Thanks," he says. A second passes, and he leans next to the counter, shifting uncomfortably. "How you holding up?"

"Me?" I ask, confused.

"Yeah, you. I know I come across all precision and military know-how, but I do have feelings, and a heart." He pauses and glances down at his feet. "We're all going through something."

He stares curiously up to me, and I can't help but think this is some cry for help, that maybe *he's* the one who needs to be asked how he is. There are so many secrets he's hiding, so many that we all are. We must remember this, especially now, now that we only have each other to rely on, that we need to be there for one another, checking in on each other.

Instead of answering his question, I ask him, "Are you okay?"

He laughs, his bright-white teeth lighting up his face, illuminating his deep dimples, the dimples I had no idea he had. "Way to change the subject."

I raise my hands in defeat. "Guilty." I laugh.

"What are you guys talking about?" Wiley says, barreling into the kitchen.

I point to Sanchez. "Sanchez was about to tell me his life story."

"No way," Wiley exclaims. "I've been prying, and he's just going to give it up easily to you?"

"No, I absolutely was not," he swears.

Wiley slaps his arm and for a slight second, it's like the world hasn't fallen apart.

Quinn and Dad walk into the room, both muttering to each other, Quinn shaking her head, Dad talking with his hands. The tension rises thick enough to shut the rest of us up.

"What's going on?" I ask.

"There seems to be some, how do I say it...consistencies." He stops for a second, thinking to himself, and follows up with, "I need more time, to test my theory."

"Sir, could you please let us know, give us some kind of insight?"

Dad shifts his weight from one foot to the other. "I don't think the virus effects are random. I don't know the connection yet, but there are similarities in Skylar's blood and the woman's blood. The man's blood and," he pauses again, glaring at Sanchez, "your blood."

Wiley chimes in, "So, it's like a guy thing and girl thing?"

"No, not that at all. See," he says, rubbing his head, "I'd rather go over this once I have more concrete info to give you."

"My blood also matched yours and the man's," Quinn gestures to Sanchez. "And Keith to Wiley."

Just like that, everyone turns to gawk at me.

"Where do I fit in?"

"That's the thing I can't quite figure out," Dad wavers, clearly perplexed.

"What do you mean you can't figure it out? What's the difference?" I say, my voice growing louder.

"I don't have enough samples to go off of at this point. It only makes sense there's an outlier. I don't know if that means we don't have a viable match to yours, or..."

"Or what? You can't just leave a sentence unfinished like that."

He looks at me, really looks at me, and replies, "Or there isn't a match."

20

———

MAX

Time has gone in slow motion since the talk in the kitchen. Because Dad refused to discuss the situation any further, we all split up. Quinn and I went to Skylar, me sitting by the bedside, holding Skylar's hand, and Quinn checking her vitals.

"I know it wasn't the news you wanted, but it really is good news," she encourages.

"How is that good news?" I ask, not meaning to come across as rude as I sound.

"It's progress. It's some type of information that we can work with, that can help us figure out what's going on."

"Yeah," I say, and even though it's incredibly frustrating not knowing what I can do with this information, she's right, at least it's something.

"Her vitals are stronger," Quinn adds.

"They are?" My mood immediately changes.

"Not dramatically but definitely an improvement. Her body needed that nourishment. I'll leave you two alone. I'll be back in a little bit to check her over again." She offers a smile, removing the cuff from Skylar's arm and placing it on the night-stand beside the bed.

Once I'm sure she's left the room, I lean down closer and speak.

"You hear that? You're doing better, Skylar. You're going to pull through this. I know it. Don't give up."

I place my lips gently on her forehead and settle into my position on the recliner.

Fighting my exhaustion, I doze in and out of consciousness. I don't know how long I've been out when the sound of the blood pressure device wakes me. I open my eyes to find Quinn standing over Skylar, finishing her checks.

"Sorry." She reveals in a whisper.

"It's okay. How long was I out?"

"Not too long. I brought you dinner." She points to the small table beside me. There sits a sandwich, some chips, and a bottle of Gatorade. "Or, well, it's more like *lunch*."

"Thanks," I say, my stomach growling in response.

She comes around the bed and with her back against the wall, slides down to a sitting position on the floor.

"You all right?" I ask, mouth full of what seems to be a turkey and cheese sandwich. Actual chunks of sliced turkey, not that stuff you get in the deli. Dad freezes everything; he must have saved leftovers from Thanksgiving or something.

"Can I tell you something?" she says, staring at me.

I wipe my mouth. "Yeah, of course." I position myself in her direction.

"I overheard Alex and your dad talking."

"Okay..." I say when she doesn't say anything else.

"Listen, I don't want to start trouble or, like, stir drama or anything, but Alex is very adamant on this whole *resistance* thing."

"What do you mean?"

"I just can't help but feel like he's becoming impatient with the whole situation here." She motions toward Skylar.

"What makes you say that?"

"Well, he literally said so. He said *I'm getting impatient with the situation.*"

"Wow."

"Right? I mean, I feel like we're making progress. And clearly, your dad isn't leaving without you, and you're not leaving without Skylar, so I don't really know what the guy expects."

"Exactly. Did you hear anything else?"

"Please don't freak out on me with what I'm about to tell you."

My heart skips a beat. I swallow down the immediate urge to panic, and somehow, with a calm demeanor, say, "Okay."

I must have been convincing because she decides to speak. "He, I mean, your dad, he thinks you may have an outlier. He wants to do more testing, as he said, but I think he's really onto something. Some of the stuff that we've discussed and hypothesized actually makes sense, and we need another body to figure it out."

And then it hits me. We have a comatose, a deranged, now we need a mind-controlled. Another question floats to the surface—are there other strains?

"What else aren't you telling me?" I ask, unable to resist the feeling that she's not telling me everything.

"I want to be completely honest and transparent with you, Max, I really do. But there's just some stuff that I think you'd freak out about. And then there's the stuff that isn't even solid, so like why bring it up, ya know?"

"I guess," I say, picking at an imaginary piece of lint. "I'm sorry that I react like an idiot sometimes." I meet her eyes. "I'm really freaking out inside. I've finally found something—someone—worth fighting for, and I'm scared, I'm really, really scared. I've known Skylar my entire life, she was my best friend growing up, and then life took her away from me. I finally got her back and I can't let it happen again."

Quinn reaches across and puts her hand on top of mine.

Only then do I realize that I had pulled apart a frayed section of my pant leg.

"I understand," she concedes.

"I don't even care if she doesn't want to *be* with me, you know. I just can't lose her again. I'll be whatever she needs me to be."

"I understand," she repeats herself.

I'm reminded of what Sanchez said to me in the kitchen, how we're all going through something. It makes me feel like a selfish idiot. Quinn would probably rather be in my position, holding on to some shred of hope instead of the fate she was dealt with Cynthia.

"I'm sorry, Quinn. I know you're going through this, too. We're all dealing with things. I hope you know I'm grateful you're here, don't forget that."

"Max," she says, blinking away the tears forming in her eyes. "He thinks your blood might be able to help her."

My eyes go wide; my heart seems to thud its way out of my chest. I'm left speechless but find myself on my feet immediately.

"I...I—ugh..." I stutter, frantically looking around in an attempt to figure out what to do.

"Please, you can't freak out. You can't even say anything," she begs.

"You expect me to not say *anything?*" I say, my hands to my face, desperately trying to rub sense into myself.

"We don't know for sure, you have to let him finish his testing. Please, he's going to be so mad at me for telling you. He knew you would react this way, I tried to reason with him, but he insisted. Please don't prove him right. Breathe, Max, breathe."

21

———

MAX

I find myself pacing the room. "How do you even know?"

"I've said it before, and I'll say it over and over, your dad, the dude really is a genius."

I stop dead in my tracks, look Quinn in the eye, and with the most serious stare I can manage, tell her, "I will walk right out this door. I will go find him. And I will prove him right."

She puts her hands up. "Okay, Okay, chill. I don't know all the details, all right? Calm down, please. I only know that he was doing some type of testing, your blood and hers, and when mixed together, there was some type of reaction."

"What do you mean, reaction? What does that even mean?"

"He got some crazy hunch, because yours didn't really match anyone else's, so he started testing it against the others. When yours and Skylar's were combined, the virus antibodies were reduced."

I don't say anything for a moment, forcing myself to process and try to understand what she's saying, what her words mean.

And then it clicks. She's saying I can save Skylar, that my blood can save her.

I turn abruptly, ready to burst out the door when Quinn grabs me.

"Stop, you have to stop!"

"Why? Why are you so desperate to keep this a secret?"

"Max, your dad wants to tell you himself, but not until he has something more concrete. I shouldn't have even said anything. It's probably some random fluke."

"How could this be a fluke?" I demand and plead for the universe to not be so cruel.

"He tested your blood with the deranged man's, and there was no reaction."

"Maybe...maybe he just didn't test it right. Maybe it doesn't work for him or something. Oh god." I fall sluggishly into the wall. "Why did you even say anything?"

"Listen, don't blame me, I'm trying to help you. I'm trying to keep you in the know. Your dad will figure something out, you have to give him some time. He's working harder than you think, day and night, desperate to figure something out."

"Yeah," is all I can manage to say. I close my eyes, head falling down in defeat. "I have to do something, I can't let her die," I say, almost in a whisper.

"I know," Quinn assures. "We need a little more time."

———

"Max." Dad startles me back to reality.

I glance up. His face is drained, lacking its normal beige tones, and he's clearly in need of a shower, or maybe a full twenty-four hours of sleep.

"Yeah?"

"Can you come with me for a minute, I have some questions?" he asks, not fatherly but perhaps doctorly.

I get up without question and follow him to the door but stop short and turn.

Quinn somehow reads my mind, following with, "I'll look after her," and walks over to Skylar's bedside. "I need to do a check of her vitals anyway."

I can't seem to bring myself to say anything to him, knowing how much it would disappoint Quinn, considering how much she begged me not to. Instead, I try to telepathically force him into telling me.

He walks me into his office and closes the door behind me. The room smells sour, almost like vinegar, mixed with iron. The far wall, typically lined with shelves of books and neatly placed trinkets, has been cleared off, and a makeshift laboratory has taken its place. A mini-fridge that was once full of my mom's wine, is now plugged in on the floor within feet of the lab. I scan the room and find my gaze falling on Dad, his hands pressed together, pondering something uncomfortable.

"I need to ask you a series of questions, and I want complete honesty, okay?" His serious tone and deadening eyes bore into me.

A fear bubbling up I was unaware I was capable of.

I nod, scared of what's to come.

"You and Jules..." he begins.

My mind does a double and triple take on his words. Why is he bringing up Jules? I lean forward a bit, in anticipation for the words to follow, completely and utterly confused. His gaze traces the floor, then moves awkwardly to meet mine.

"You were *careful,* right?"

The way he enunciates *careful* makes me realize why he's so uncomfortable.

"Gross, Dad, what the hell?"

His face remains the same, stern but uncomfortable. "Just answer the question, please."

"Yes, I mean, no, it wasn't, ugh...necessary. Next question, please."

He looks at me, studying my response and the space in between, deciding whether or not to accept my answer.

I cock my head a little to the side, silently asking him for the next question.

"Any drug use?"

"Dad, seriously?"

"Yes, I am very serious," he echoes, straight-faced. "These questions are painfully as awkward for me as they are for you, but I need to know the answers."

"Okay, fine, sorry. No, no drug use."

"None? Not weed, pills, anything with a needle?" he asks in more detail.

"Only those pain pills you gave me," I say defensively.

"And that's it?" he questions fiercely.

"Yes, Dad, I swear. No drugs, I don't even drink. That was Jake who stole your scotch, not me," I say all at once, trying to make him understand.

"Okay." He rubs his chin. "And you're a relatively healthy young man." He pauses for a second. "How are you feeling? Any flu-like symptoms, allergies or fever?" He takes a step forward, putting the back of his hand on my forehead. He reaches down and puts his hand around my wrist, turning it over and placing two fingers to find my pulse; he finds the clock across the room and stares blankly.

I remind myself not to hold my breath, waiting for him to finish.

"I feel fine. Are you going to tell me what this is all about?" I pry but try not to come across overbearing.

He chews at the inside of his lip, and it's almost as if I can see the wheels turning in his head, connecting pieces to a puzzle no one can see, solving problem after problem, what he does best.

"I need some more blood samples, from everyone, and I need to make sure of certain things before taking any unnecessary risks." He's lying.

Even if Quinn hadn't told me the truth, I would be able to tell through this lie. That whole, father/son thing we have. We've lived on our own long enough to be able to pick up these cues from each other, which is probably why he believed my responses about Jules and drugs.

"Okay." I allow him to think he fooled me. "Whatever you need." I take a step toward the lab area. "Should we do it now?"

"Yeah, good idea to get it out of the way now. Thanks for being understanding. I think I'm making some progress, I just need bigger samples to work with." Lies on lies. Well, part of it. What he is saying *is* true, just not in the way he's implying.

"Of course, whatever I can do to help."

He motions for me to take a seat, and I comply.

"What type of progress are you making?" I ask, hoping for something that resembles the truth.

"You know me, not a big teller until I have something solid."

He fakes a smile, and even though he may be telling the truth, I know he's withholding something.

Tension, radiating the space between us, sets my nerves all the more on edge when he brings the supplies and places them on the small table beside me. I find a picture to occupy my attention in the far corner, a beautiful x-ray flower. The petals are gorgeously translucent, in various shades of purple, and the stem, a deep forest green, both perfectly laced together—clearly a piece of artwork chosen by my mom. Glancing around, I see that the picture is really the only thing of much color in the office. Everything else is either shades of white and gray, or wood tones.

"Going to take a few extra of these this time." He waves an empty vial in front of my face for me to see.

It pains me to think of her—my mom—but it pains me, even more, to think about all the time that has passed since she's been gone, how life managed to continue after her absence. How this world didn't deserve her, but how desperately empty life is without her.

"Hey, hold this right here for me, will you?"

I reach down and hold the contraption in place, an empty vial filling with my blood. He runs to a cabinet in the corner of his office. He opens the small door, and I look down to see a few of the vials he had taken of my blood, and before I can even process what I'm doing, I glance quickly to him and seize the opportunity to snatch one and put it in my pocket.

"Shit," I exclaim, biting my lip to keep quiet. In the midst of me stealing a vial of my own blood, I had let go of the device drawing my blood. The needle moved and jammed itself painfully in a weird position.

Dad jerks his head around quickly, slamming shut the cabinet door as he comes to my aid. "And that right there is why Max Sinclair will not be a doctor," he laughs, seemingly unaware of the missing vial.

Within seconds, he's removed the device and secured a cotton ball with the medical tape he took from the cabinet.

"Need anything else?" I ask.

"Not right now, buddy. Thanks." He clutches my shoulder and gives it a firm squeeze. "You doing okay?" And somehow, the lying, misleading man has been replaced with my father and finds a home inside me.

"Yeah, I'm all right," I lie.

"Go check on Quinn. We'll talk in a little bit, okay?"

And with that, I'm on the other side of his office door, standing in the hallway, hand wrapped around the warm vial in my pocket, unsure of what I'm doing next, but knowing I have to do something, anything.

22

MAX

When I reach the doorway to my room, I quickly dart inside.

"Oh god, you scared me. I didn't think you'd still be here," I stutter.

She eyes me suspiciously. "You know, guilty people scare easily."

I blankly stare at her, the temperature of my body rising. She knows I've done something, but how?

"So...?" she says, in anticipation for my response.

I swallow hard, fumbling on the vial in my pocket. If I tell her, she can help me figure out what to do with it, how to use it, how to help her.

"I, ugh—" I trail off, not able to form a sentence. *Just tell her, you idiot.*

She sighs heavily. "Is he super pissed at me?"

Her response catches me off guard. "What?" I ask reflexively.

"What is *wrong* with you? You told your dad, right? You told him what I told you?" And that's the moment I realize that she has no idea what's in my pocket, she's just worried I told him.

I shake my head, probably too much. "No, no, no, I didn't say anything."

She squints and tilts her head. "You didn't?"

"No." I shake my head again.

"Then why are you being so strange?" she asks.

Shit. Hurry up and think of a cover.

"He, ugh, he drew my blood. You know how I get with needles." *Smooth one.*

"Oh, right, yeah, that makes sense." She glares at me like she's pondering my response. "Okay." She stands from the chair, wiping her hands on her legs, and walks toward me, on her way to the door. "You," she pokes me in the chest, "are being weirder than normal."

I offer a fake smile. "I'm just tired, I think."

"Uh-huh, whatever." She takes her leave.

I shut the door quietly, leaving only a small crack, and tiptoe closer to the bed, feeling almost as if I'm not meant to be in here.

I sit on the bed and let out a heavy exhale, allowing my shoulders to slump. I take my hand away from the vial in my pocket and rub my fingers into my forehead. I have to weigh my options. What even are my options? I really don't know what I'm doing. But I know that my blood could possibly help her. I know that a tiny bit of my blood, mixed with a tiny bit of her blood, somehow reacted together. Something about antibodies.

Maybe if I got this vial of blood inside her, it could do the same thing. But how do I do that? I shift my weight and glare at the contraptions attached to Skylar.

"Oh, you poor sweet girl," I say. "You don't deserve this."

The small tube feeding her the nutrients she needs to survive, trails from her nose, taped to the side of her cheek. An

IV hooked to her arm is attached to fluids that I assume are keeping her hydrated.

My mind wanders to what my dad had asked Quinn, intra-something or intra-muscular. He was talking about how she injected the man with the sedative. When she answered intra-something, he had given her an attagirl, meaning that was the preferred way of injection. I'm fairly certain what they meant was either in a vein or a random injection. I can't imagine that injecting this blood right into Skylar would be effective, so I have to figure out how to get it directly into a vein.

I look to the IV attached to her arm. I guess I could take off the attached lines and use that, but it seems complicated, and I don't really know how I would attach the vial. Not to mention, I don't know what's in the IV, and I don't want to take away any vital nutrient or life support.

Quinn's backpack catches my attention, tucked partially under the bed near my feet. I lean over, tug it out, and right on top in sealed packaging is a brand-new syringe. My heart skips a beat, and after a quick glance over my shoulder, I grab the package and put it in my pocket with the vial.

My eyes go wide. What am I doing? I have to do something. I can't continue to wait around doing nothing. I can't let another moment go by without at least trying.

I put the vial and syringe package on the bed between Skylar and me, and then reach across to the bedside table and pump a heap of sanitizer into my palm. The alcohol burns my eyes and singes all the tiny cuts on my fingers I didn't know I had. I put on a pair of latex gloves from the box on the night-stand, take another peek at the door and open the syringe package.

My hands shake, and I force myself to take a breath. I allow barely a fraction of a second to get my crap together. Examination of the vial shows a miniscule hole in the middle of the top, so I shove the needle of the syringe into the vial and move back the plunger, filling the syringe with blood. I pull the syringe out, holding it up to the light, and, doing the thing I always see in the movies, I flick the barrel a bit and squeeze gently until a teeny bit of blood dribbles from the tip of the needle.

With the syringe in one hand, I turn to Skylar, fear washing over me with the realization I have no idea what I'm doing. I take my free hand to feel around on her arm, right above the ditch of her elbow. Somehow, the gods are on my side, because a lump of a vein sticks out saying *hello, here I am!*

Without thinking anymore, I bring the syringe closer to her arm, feeling one last time to make sure the vein is there, and ever so gently, press the needle into her. Nausea hits me like a ton of bricks, but I force myself to see this through. I press the plunger and gradually empty the contents of the vial into her vein—my blood.

I slap the syringe onto the table and fall to my knees beside her. She lies there, unmoving, unchanged, like nothing has happened and that I didn't, mere seconds ago, inject my blood into her. I stare at her intensely, waiting for the slightest infraction. I press her hand against my forehead and suppress the tears welling in my eyes, fighting their way to the front. What have I done? What if this was all for nothing? What if I harmed her even more? I'm so stupid. This was so stupid. I was selfish. I should have never been so careless, so irresponsible and reckless.

A noise from the door flickers in my ear, but I refuse to acknowledge it. Shuffling feet follow the person entering the room.

Her voice is quiet, angelic even. "Are you asleep?" she asks. "That looks uncomfortable."

"No." I sniffle.

"Are you okay?" she says while coming closer. And then it's

like she sees or senses or telepathically knows. "Max..." Her voice grows. "What did you do?"

"I just wanted to help," I say, defeated.

"Move," she snaps. "I need you to move, right now."

I stay put, unmovable.

She grabs something off the table and nudges me with her hip, pressing into the space between me and Skylar.

Air, being squeezed, a sound I recognize as a blood pressure cuff. Seconds passing, feeling both like an eternity and like its spiraling out of control so quickly I can't catch up.

"Holy shit," she mutters under her breath.

I'm too afraid to look up, to face the reality of what I've done. I've never not wanted to exist so badly in my life. It's not a feeling of wanting to die more than it is of just wanting to go away, to be wiped off the planet, never to have been there to begin with. That all of my actions could be erased, the words I've said, unspoken. Maybe those around me would be better off. I shut myself into the deepest darkest part of me I can find.

"I have to go get Keith, just...just stay here, okay?"

A million things run through my head, but the realization that I've put Skylar in more danger, that my actions can't be undone, settles a weight on me I can't bear to handle. The sound of Quinn rushing out of the room brings me back to my senses, and before I can even process what I'm doing, I'm in the hallway, and my feet are at the front door, and my hand is on the knob, and I'm turning it, and I'm outside.

The sky burns vibrant shades of reds and purples, the sun setting on the horizon, something I would have once stopped and gawked at but now feel no satisfaction in its glory. An ache deepens in my chest and weaves its way through every fiber of my being.

I walk, I walk so blindly and unknowing until I can't see the light from the cabin. The tears that I can no longer fight make their way eagerly, cascading down each cheek. I bite the inside of my lip, blood pooling in my mouth, and the sensation brings me enough control to stop the tears from flowing.

I slump against a tree and slide down until my butt is planted in the dirt.

I don't have the will to go any farther, figuratively or literally.

23

QUINN

I don't know how he did it. How he managed to steal a vial of his own blood. How he snuck it past his dad, how he snuck it past me. How he got the supplies he needed. How he figured out how to even get a vein, and how he managed to properly inject Skylar with his blood. Especially considering he's such a baby about needles.

He was incredibly stupid, selfish, and absolutely reckless.

I should have known better given he was being super weird. I had a hunch that something was wrong, that something wasn't sitting right. But I believed his lie about being tired and woozy from getting his blood drawn again.

I was stupid for just letting that go, and now here I am, frantically searching the wooded area around the cabin to try to find him.

Keith stayed with Skylar, and with Wiley somehow asleep already, Alex and I took off after Max. Alex decided we should split up, so each of us armed with a flashlight went in separate directions from the house.

My only instruction from Alex being, "Don't go too far, it's not worth getting lost."

But I find myself feeling the opposite. The relationship Max and I have developed over the last couple of weeks has been such a welcome surprise. At first, he hated me, or, well, I guess I took his massive ignoring me as hatred. But then something broke inside him, and ever since that moment, our friendship has deepened. Loss will do that to you, it will break you, it will tear you apart, and it will form bonds with unlikely people.

Max is like the brother I never had. The really idiotic but genuinely caring brother.

And maybe it's my desire to fix everyone else because I can't fix myself that makes me desperate to find him.

His love for Skylar is immense, passionate and raw. The relationship he and his dad share, the bond he has with Wiley—I'd be lying if I said I wasn't envious, but that's what drives me to help him; he has so much to live for, to be proud of and fight for. Even if I'm on the sidelines and play the smallest role, it would be nice to know I helped him hold on to the things and people he loves.

"Max," I whisper loudly, a contradiction in itself. "Where are you, you idiot?"

The illumination from my flashlight shines fiercely, brightening up the darkness of night, showing me infinite rows of trees. My hope fades, and the realization that he could be anywhere consumes me heavily. I take a deep breath, check both left and right, and decide to put myself in his shoes and go straight.

The forest at night fills all of my senses, the chatter of bugs in the distance, the thick smell of mud and fallen branches, the bright leaf-covered trees igniting from my flashlight. My eyes are a constant flutter, shifting from the ground directly in front of me, to ahead, to along the base of trees.

A faint sound stands out from the rest, and I can't seem to place it. Cautiously but quickly, I move in its direction. I hear it again and I'm drawn toward it. Something streaks across the ground in the distance, and I assume Alex is making his way toward the sound, too.

I pick up my pace and jog toward the sound and flickering, and as I approach, Alex grab's Max's shoulder and pulls him abruptly off the ground. Max appears surprised and tries to rip his shoulder away.

"Don't be a child," Alex demands. "You're wasting all of our time. We're going back to the cabin."

"I'm not going anywhere with you," Max replies.

I reach the two of them, and Max avoids my eyes, staring at nothing in particular on the ground.

"Hey now, calm down, Alex," I say, trying to remove his hand from Max.

"We're wasting time. Why does no one seem to care we're wasting time?"

"Just give me a second with him," I plead.

"Whatever, you deal with him," he huffs and storms off toward our temporary home.

Without breaking his concentration on the ground, Max grumbles, "I'm sorry."

He sniffles, the familiar sound much louder and apparent now that I'm right next to it.

"Listen, it'll be okay, but we really need to go," I say.

"I can't, I can't go. Not there. Not after this." He shakes his head.

"Max," I say, trying to get his attention.

"No, I can't. I won't go back."

"Max, you have to listen to me." I grab his arm, shake him a little. "Look at me."

He glances up, his eyes bloodshot, the remnants of tears

dried against his cheeks. My heart breaks a little for him, and I realize he must not understand.

"Don't make me go there, not right now."

"It's going to be okay, Max, she's going to be okay."

"You don't know that." He raises his voice slightly, almost becoming delirious.

"You don't understand. You helped her. Please, come to the cabin with me so I can show you."

Suddenly, his eyes darken and come alive, and he speaks in a rush. "What? What do you mean? You're lying." His desperate gaze shifts toward the cabin and returns to me.

"I can't really explain. We haven't made any sense of it yet. Your dad is doing some tests, but listen, whatever you did, it *helped*. So please just listen to me, we need to get back."

He stares at me in a way that terrifies me.

"You're not lying?"

"No, I wouldn't lie to you about this. Can we please go now?"

"God, I'm such an idiot, I thought..."

"Yeah, you sure are an idiot." I laugh.

"Wait, so she's better? What are we waiting on? Come on." He bolts away, leaving me behind in a cloud of dust.

It takes me a second to process that he's gone, and when I do, I take off after him. I try to catch up, but he sprints ahead, and considering his legs are a heck of a lot longer than mine, he covers much more ground than I can.

He barrels through the front door, and it takes me another minute to catch up. When I reach the steps, I'm out of breath, my heart pounding feverishly, and my pulse heavy all over my body, thudding loudly in my ears.

I go inside to find the sound of my heartbeat being drowned out by voices. Multiple people talking over one another. I drop my flashlight on the table by the door and make my way toward them, entering Max's bedroom.

"Max, what you did was incredibly stupid," Keith says.

I swallow down the lump forming in my throat and lean into the wall, willing myself to become invisible while a dad rips a son's ass.

24

———

MAX

I clear the steps to the cabin in one leap and am through the front door and into my bedroom in record speed. I come around the edge of the bed, and Dad nearly jumps out of his skin.

"What the hell were you thinking?" he demands.

"How is she?"

"You had no right, no right to do this, and no right to idiotically take off like that. Tell me what the hell you were thinking."

"You really need to ask what I was thinking? I had to do something. You won't tell me anything. You and Quinn go and run your tests and keep the results to yourself. When were you going to tell *me*, huh?"

It was never like this, the whole keeping secrets from each other thing. My dad and I have always been close, and even closer following Mom's death. We had to be, we were all we had left. Our family stretches across the coast of California and Florida, and once the dust settled of my mom dying, no one really kept in contact anymore. It was like we were long forgotten. Wiley became our family and held together the pieces of brokenness in our time of need. The relationship my dad and I shared became closer than ever. There were the things we didn't talk about, but not because we wanted to keep them secret, but because we're guys and don't gossip and talk feelings.

Stuff like whether or not my blood could help the girl I love should definitely be on the list of stuff we talk about. This is a definite need-to-know thing. And the fact that he just didn't tell me is unacceptable. Even if he didn't know for sure, he could have told me. I'd rather him be open and honest than keep things from me.

"What are you talking about?" he asks, pretending to be confused.

"You know what I'm talking about. My blood. I'm not stupid, you know."

"You are, though. You really are. Max, what you did was incredibly stupid."

"You never used to keep things from me, Dad. Why wouldn't you just tell me?"

"I didn't want to get your hopes up, okay? I know you and Skylar have some intense bond, you always have, since you were born you two shared something. And honestly, I can only imagine how this feels, finally getting her back after all these years and then having her ripped away again. I didn't want to get your hopes up. I was trying to protect you."

"I'm not a child anymore," I snap. "You have no right." My head shakes and I point my finger furiously. "No right to not tell me things *this* important."

The anger bubbles up from somewhere deep inside, anger mixed with heartbreak and frustration and deceit. My jaw clenches, and a small hand touching my arm startles me.

"Remember our talk?" Quinn pleads quietly but desperately. Her cobalt eyes sparkle as they bore into me.

It's then that I do remember. She told me he thought I would freak out, that he wanted to wait until he had something more concrete. They were afraid I would act irrationally.

They were right.

I stole my own blood, I injected it into Skylar in a frantic and completely foolish attempt to help, to do something.

I was stupid, and here I am treating Dad like garbage for not telling me, for doing the thing he thought was right given my slightly reckless behavior around Skylar. Slightly might be the understatement of the year. She blinds me, makes me feel and think and act in ways I didn't think I was capable. Not always in bad ways, but the thought of losing the good is creating this monster that will stop at nothing to save her.

"Yeah."

She smiles and I'm surprised to find it calming the demon in me. I don't know what I did to deserve her kindness, her friendship. Especially considering the circumstances. I would want nothing to do with me, but she manages to hold on to some shred of my humanity, keeping me afloat while I struggle through this nightmare.

My eyes close, and when they open, I exhale, finding myself somehow more relaxed, pushing away the tension.

"I'm sorry," I offer.

Dad rubs his temple. "Listen, I get it. I know this is hard, and I'm sorry for not being more open, but I'm just trying to protect you. Not give you false hope." He swallows hard. "I've been there, holding on to every ounce of hope..." His eyes glaze, staring aimlessly off into the distance. Then, snapping back to reality, he continues, "I'll try to be better with telling you things, as long as you do your best to not freak out on me. I'm trying, okay? Trust me, Skylar is important to me, too."

"That's all I ask, thank you." The sincerity feeling somewhat real in his words lifts a tiny invisible weight from my shoulders.

Quinn interjects, "Good, glad that's cleared up. Now, on to more pressing matters." She motions to the sleeping beauty lying in my bed.

"Right, yes. Well, initially, her vitals have improved but seem to be at a bit of a standstill. I'll have to run further analysis to determine a more solid conclusion, but we seem to be onto something. I'd like to run another sample of her blood against yours, Max. I'm not an expert on these matters, so this is a bit of a learning curve." He frowns slightly. "But, nothing we can't figure out." He nudges Quinn. "You make a great partner."

"That's good, though, right?" I ask, trying not to sound overly hopeful.

"To have any type of lead in this foreign situation is definitely good. Obviously, nutrition helped, but only so much. The medication we've tried hasn't seemed to make any difference. To see an actual improvement of any kind is great. Now it's only a matter of figuring out the how and why, and how to amplify those results. I know it may seem like a good idea to just inject her with mass quantities of your blood, that isn't necessarily a feasible option for either of you, so please for the love of everything holy, do *not* do that."

I raise my hands in surrender. "Okay, I won't, but it does seem like a good idea from over here."

Quinn speaks up. "Medically speaking, not knowing what we're dealing with in Skylar's blood, not even knowing if she's a proper recipient or how her body will react in the next twenty-four hours to the amount of blood that's in her system now, it's a horrible idea."

"That makes sense," I respond.

"So, on that note, I know time isn't really on our side, but we need to let this marinate a bit. See what happens, at least overnight. Quinn will stay consistent with checking her vitals, and I'll be busy plugging away in my makeshift lab. Can you handle that?" Dad asks.

I observe a sort of gentleness I had almost forgot existed within him.

"Yeah, I can handle that."

"Good," he says. "Now, I'm trusting you, Max, nothing crazy. And you," he points to Quinn, "keep an eye on him. I have work to do, and I can't have you in here running some half-assed transfusion."

As the last word rolls out of his mouth, I watch him mentally check himself out of the room, running data like he does, not always obvious to those around him but obvious to the observant son standing in front of him.

"You okay?" Quinn asks him, clearly confused about why he abruptly stopped talking.

"Huh, yeah, sorry," he declares and then smiles. "Had an idea."

"Let me guess." I roll my eyes. "You won't tell me."

He points at me and laughs. "You are correct, son. But, don't worry, I'll let you know in the morning if I make any progress, deal?"

"Fine, deal, but I'm serious. If you somehow figure out how to fix all of this, please freaking tell me, or at least tell Quinn so then she can tell me."

"Hey, leave me out of this. I'm never telling you anything again," she jokes, shoving me slightly.

"All right, be good, I'm super serious. How many times do I have to say I'm serious before you behave?"

He leaves the room, the air already feeling lighter, the tension lessened following our sort of argument.

Once I make sure he's down the hall, I turn to Quinn and quietly ask, "You saw that, right, his weirdness after he said something about a transfusion?"

25

———

MAX

Morning slowly rolls in, each second antagonizing and painful. I wait eagerly in anticipation for whatever update Dad might be able to provide. I barely slept, dozing in and out of consciousness, hopeful that maybe, just maybe he would burst through the door any moment and tell me he figured out how to save Skylar, how to bring her back.

The clock on the nightstand reads 6:08 a.m., and I know soon that the house will begin to stir—people will wake, have breakfast, and start forming a plan for the day.

Footsteps permeate the hall and then make their way into my bedroom.

"Hey, you," Dad says, almost cheerful.

My heart decides to do a flip, anxiously catapulting itself.

"Hey," I manage to respond.

"Quinn will be in shortly," he says, approaching Skylar's side, notebook in hand.

"Is everything okay?" I ask, a sinking feeling taking hold. My palms fill with a light dusting of sweat.

He smiles. "Yeah. Don't worry, I wanted to go over things together, instead of individually, saves time."

An eternity passes, or maybe a minute, and Quinn finally enters.

"Morning, fellas," she says, towel drying her freshly showered hair.

"Glad you were able to find some of Maura's old clothes that fit. I could never bring myself to get rid of them. It's nice to know they're coming in handy now."

"I had to do a little digging; that woman has way more style than I do." She laughs. "I really appreciate it, thank you, Keith."

I clear the log that has formed in my throat. "So, what's the update?"

"Right, Mr. Impatient over here," he chuckles and winks at me. "So, get this, after further analysis, there is most definitely a reaction with your blood and Skylar's, and your blood with the woman's, but here's where it gets weird—no reaction with the man we're claiming is deranged. I tested all of the rest of our blood against the two, and there was no positive reaction. Quinn's and Sanchez's blood both drastically mutated whatever virus is present from the deranged man's blood, leading me to assume that had they been infected, they would show signs of being deranged." He pauses, perhaps allowing this information to sink in.

Quinn speaks first. "How does Max's blood factor in here, and yours and Wiley's?"

"Well, mine and Wiley's had no positive effect on Skylar's. And even though Max's did, it deems to be only temporary."

"What do you mean, temporary?" I say, clearly speaking out of turn.

"It's almost as if your blood acts as just a bandage, helping, but not necessarily fixing the problem."

My heart seems to shatter, the hope of thinking I could help in some way swept out from under me.

"Oh," I say, shrunken and defeated. I must have misread his smile from when he entered the room and his excitement last night of whatever theory he had thought.

"The immune response is incredible, really. Your blood alone basically attacks what bits of Skylar's blood is injected, in small quantities obviously. Being such a small sample, it's a manageable volume, but as a whole, to send minimal amounts of your blood into *Skylar's* isn't feasible."

Looking to the floor, Quinn rubs her hands and then seemingly allows her gaze to wander the room at nothing in particular, lost in thought. "You weren't thinking transfusion." She says it as both a question and a statement, more so like she's wanting clarification.

"No." He shakes his head.

My gaze locks on her, then on him, then Quinn once more.

"Someone tell me what's going on, please," I beg. "I can't read between the lines of whatever medical mumbo jumbo you're telepathically talking to each other about."

Completely ignoring me, she asks Dad, "Is it even possible?"

"Is what possible?" I ask frantically.

"In theory, yes. But there are numerous hypotheticals, different variables we need to consider," he responds.

"The first of which is whether she's even a recipient. The magnitude of that alone could pose great risks, even being potentially fatal."

"Not only is Skylar a recipient, but they're both young, healthy. Well, given the circumstances."

"Is this even possible? Could we even pull this off?" Quinn stares at Dad while he stares bug-eyed back.

"Is *what* possible? Someone tell me what the *hell* is going on?" I demand.

Acting as though I've only just entered the room, they both face me.

Quinn declares. "Okay, so sit down."

"No, tell me what's going on. What are you talking about? You two are making no sense."

Quinn looks to Dad. "Do you want to explain this or should I?"

Dad begins, "This is probably going to make no sense, so I'll try my best to simplify it for you. Heck, I don't even really know all the technical terms myself." He laughs.

I don't see the humor whatsoever.

"I'll try where I can," Quinn chimes in.

"Think of it this way. You have a dirty bucket, and it needs to be cleaned. You try to pour clean water in the bucket of the dirt, but it solely isn't enough to clean it without getting dirty again. So, you filter the dirt and water through a secondary source, like a hose, that self-cleans at a greater rate, and in return, end up replacing the nasty water with clean."

"You're right, even dumbed down I'm not following," I say.

Quinn shakes her head. "Okay, listen, Skylar is the dirty blood. You are the clean blood, aka the hose. The clean water, aka blood that we inject, isn't coming in at a great enough rate to clean her before the virus mutates, so we manage a direct filtering system, siphoning her blood through you, replacing her bad blood with your good blood."

"Deal, sign me up."

"You're not concerned with what happens to your blood?"

"What happens to my blood?"

"Well, the bad blood that enters your system, your body will fight and basically clean and replenish what you're giving her."

"Great. I don't see the problem," I say, glancing at both of them. "When do we start?"

Quinn smirks at Dad. "I guess consent isn't going to be an issue then."

Dad speaks with precision. "Max, you need to think about this for more than a second. We really have no idea what we're doing here. This is a *theory*. A really probable theory, but still. This could pose a threat to both of you."

"Look, save your breath, I don't really want the whole speech. The *stop and think about it* speech. I get it. This is dangerous. I can't imagine either one of you has ever done this procedure, let alone us having the proper supplies. I understand the risks. I accept them. I cannot accept just sitting here and doing nothing. We have to do *something*. And if this is the something, then we do it. Just tell me what I need to do. I refuse to have an option and not try." I pause for a second and add, "I trust both of you."

The words slip out of my mouth with ease, even though I'm scared as hell inside. Scared this might not work, scared it might make things somehow worse. I can't let fear get in the way of doing something that might actually help. The fear of losing Skylar is greater than any other fear I've known.

26
———

MAX

I stand there, waiting for some type of response, but am met with Dad and Quinn just sort of looking at each other dumbfounded. They had to have expected I would easily say yes. It's what I do—I make irrational, immediate decisions, especially if I think it could help someone, not to mention that someone being Skylar. And maybe it's not whether they expected me to say yes, but whether they think this is actually irrational and stupid. Maybe they were desperately hoping I would say no, so they wouldn't be bothered rationalizing this seemingly impossible task.

Maybe I should have said no, maybe I should take some time to think this through. Maybe I should be more concerned with the risks, the dangers I would be putting myself through, putting Skylar through.

But I don't. All I can think about are the dead around us. The ticking time bomb that is death, creeping its way closer to Skylar. The woman in the bait shop that I witnessed give her last breath. That could be Skylar, and it could be any moment.

"Morning, everyone," a thick manly voice speaks.

Dad and Quinn let out a collective 'morning' while I continue to gawk, unfazed by Sanchez as he walks closer.

"Any progress?" Sanchez asks.

"No," Dad says abruptly, his dishonesty catching me off guard.

"Oh," Sanchez replies, visibly disappointed. "I thought you were onto something last night, Keith. You were up nearly all night working, weren't you?" His question feels forced and obtrusive.

"For a minute, yes. I fell asleep in my lab, though."

Intuition is telling me this is partly a lie. Why is he lying to Sanchez? Why the secrets? There are so many unanswered questions I have yet to ask Dad, so many things that seemingly don't add up.

"Huh, okay then. Well, we should really regroup soon. Time is of the essence. We have important work to do." He raises the steaming cup of coffee in Dad's direction while offering an awkward smile, and then makes his way out of the room.

"That was...uncomfortable," Quinn says quietly.

"What the hell was that about?" I ask Dad.

"Sorry," Dad whispers. "I'm just in no hurry to tell him that my son's blood could potentially save us all."

"Understandable," Quinn says.

"How are we going to pull this off then?" I say, trying to keep my voice low. "This guy practically lives with us."

Dad scratches his head. "I guess we're going to have to make this room somehow off-limits."

"What about the risk for the virus being airborne? And quarantining the room?" Quinn suggests.

"That's a good idea," I add.

"He knows too much, though. Way more than he's letting

on. We really should talk about this privately, somewhere he can't hear," Dad insists.

As much as I want to be a part of this conversation, I can't fathom the idea of all three of us leaving Skylar alone. "I don't feel comfortable leaving her," I say, attention trailing over Skylar. "It would probably be easier for only two of us to get away than all three."

"You're right," Quinn admits. "But you sort of need to be involved, Max. This is your life on the line, too."

Dad nods.

Without allowing him to answer, I say, "You two are the brains of this operation. Just let me know what you figure out. I'll keep him in the house. Go figure something out."

"Okay..." Quinn says, clearly unconvinced.

I start to push them out of the room and an idea strikes me.

"Actually, hold on. Give me one minute, I'll be right back," I tell them.

They exchange confused looks but, not allowing them to interject, I bolt out the door.

I'm almost to the stairs when I catch a peep of him in the peripheral of my vision.

Wiley.

He nearly jumps as I clear the space between us.

Out of breath, I say, "Hey, I need a favor."

"What's up?" he asks, sleepy-eyed with a mouth full of a bagel.

Lowering my voice, I do a once-over of the room. "Where's Sanchez?"

He wipes at his mouth with his napkin. "I think he said he was going to shower or something. Why?"

"This is going to sound strange, but I need you to keep him occupied."

He scrunches his eyebrows. "What like, in the shower?" He

chuckles and picks up his mug, taking a sip of his way-too-sweet coffee. Wiley is a little-coffee-with-his-sugar kind of guy.

"No, not in the shower, you weirdo." I lightly smack his arm. "I mean, I need you to keep him in the house until I give the go-ahead, okay?"

"What's this about? Where's your dad?"

"We just need a tiny bit of time for Quinn and Dad to talk. Can you please just keep him occupied?"

"Yeah, sure, whatever. But I want the details soon, too."

"Thank you, you're a lifesaver." I grip his shoulder firmly and then walk away. In a whisper so he can't hear, I add, "Literally."

I'm almost out of the room when he asks, "Is everything okay?"

I turn quickly on my heel and grin wide. "Yeah, everything is okay."

"Holy shit," he exclaims. "Haven't seen you smile in ages. Not a bad look, kid."

"Thanks," I say, making my leave.

For the first time in a while, my heart feels light. I feel light. Like I'm floating on a cloud of puppies. The calm, rational side of me knows how foolish it is to get my hopes up, but the desperate, hopelessly in love side of me is pleading with the universe to please let this work. Let this bring Skylar back, let this rid her of whatever hell she's been forced to endure. To let me be the one to make this sacrifice for her, to do everything in my power to help, even if I must suffer, too, because I can't imagine any amount of physical pain could be any worse than what I've already been feeling.

I will do this, and I will have no regrets. I made her a promise to protect her, and I can't break that, not now, not ever.

27

———

MAX

I practically have a heart attack when Sanchez barges into my bedroom.

"Sorry, sir. I didn't mean to scare you. Where's your dad?"

Ugh, Wiley, hello, where are you?

The lump of lies forming in my throat makes it difficult to swallow. I don't dare look away from Skylar, her face a little less pale than usual. "I don't know." I shrug. "Did you ask Wiley?"

He shakes his head. "Not yet." In my peripheral, he motions toward Skylar. "So, any updates?"

He's prying, and way more than normal. He's up to something.

I shrug again, a nervous tick I can't seem to stop. "They don't really tell me anything."

"That was a real stupid move, running off like that. I'm not here to tell you how to live your life, but that kind of behavior will get you killed really fast."

"I know, I'm sorry."

"Don't apologize to me. You could have gotten Quinn hurt,

too. She ran out of the house after you. Your decisions don't only affect you, you know?"

Just then, Wiley pokes his head into the room. "Alex, hey, I've been looking for you."

Sanchez, or Alex as everyone else seems to be calling him, lets out a sigh and turns to face Wiley. "What for?"

Wiley brings his hands out from behind him, revealing a partially dismantled gun. He manages to spit out a few words, "I was trying to figure out how to take this—"

Alex cuts him off, "Whoa, whoa, what did you do? Put that thing down."

"What, I just..." Wiley is seemingly oblivious to the grown man panicking in front of him. Pure genius on Wiley's behalf. He winks at me and adds, "I just wanted to figure out how to clean it."

I hold in a laugh, not knowing Wiley had it in him to be so convincing.

"You can't go taking guns apart around here like this. Here, give me that," he demands. "Come on. I'll show you the right way to clean a gun." He shakes his head and leaves the room.

I wink at Wiley and mouth, "Thank you."

I catch sight of Skylar's notebook on the bedside table. I find myself hoping that maybe soon I won't have to hang on to this only lifeline I have of Skylar, that she'll return and be able to articulate her own words for me to consume instead of me invading her thoughts. I'm sure this will end up with her being super pissed at me for reading some of her journal entries, but I'll take her pissed at me over this any day.

I press her hand up to my face, gently resting my lips against her bare knuckles.

"Hold on a little longer," I tell her tenderly. "This could all be over soon. Dad and Quinn have a plan, and I'll do whatever it takes to get you back." I exhale deeply. "I'm so sorry for all of this, you didn't deserve this, Skylar. Whenever this is all said and done, I hope you know I never meant for this to happen. Even before *this*, the arguing, being against one another. I hope you'll know that you can trust me, to be here for you, to protect you, to be the person you need me to be. Whatever that may be. I believe in us, in you. I hope you'll believe in me, too."

———

An agonizingly long hour goes by until the front door creaks open. Footsteps fill the space, and then Quinn and Dad make their way into my bedroom.

Quinn divulges. "It's not pretty, but we think we have a plan." She falters for a second. "Have you eaten?"

"No, why?"

"You need to get your strength up, we start soon."

My eyes sway to Dad. He's beaming and nodding, and I find myself smiling, too.

"Soon, soon?"

"Yep," he marvels cheerfully.

"What, how?" I ask, feeling like an idiot for not knowing the plan already. But also incredibly excited to get this show on the road. The moment I've been waiting for, what we've all been hopeful for.

Pointing to me, Dad prompts, "Breakfast, now."

Once in the kitchen area, Alex glances up from his spot overlooking Wiley. His eyes focus on all of us, almost like he's trying to analyze us somehow.

"Hey, Keith, I was trying to find you. Well, before Wiley dismantled his gun."

Dad's eyebrows shoot up. "He did what?"

"My thoughts exactly. Anyway, we really need to sit down and chat. Figure out how to move forward."

I rummage through the fridge and try my best to listen intently.

"I agree, I actually needed to speak to you, too."

"Yeah? What's going on?" Alex replies.

"I just need more pieces to the puzzle, and I was hoping that you could help me with that."

Intrigued, Alex says, "How so?"

"Right now, we have a deranged and comatose, but if you're saying the mind-controlled are another version of this virus, then I need a blood sample from one of them, too." Despite knowing that this is part of the plan to get him out of the house, I can't help but feel like he's speaking the truth, too, that he really does need a mind-controlled blood sample.

"Good, I like the sound of that," Alex beams enthusiastically. "Anything to gain some forward momentum. It's early, we could leave soon."

I peel back the plastic on a cheese stick, and he shoots me an eager yet hopeful glare. "Max, you down to go on another adventure?"

Oh god. Shit. What do I say? I'm terrible at being called out on the spot. I panic and shove the mozzarella into my mouth, desperately hoping someone will say something, *anything*.

"I, ugh," I say between chewing, "I don't know. I don't really..."

Please, *someone*, say something.

Wiley shuffles in his seat, raising his hand and speaking first. "I'll go."

Alex frowns. "What about you, Quinn?"

She hesitates and then confidently declares, "I should really keep an eye on Skylar, especially after the recent events."

"Keith?" He's pleading at this point, anyone but Wiley.

"I'm afraid I can't step away from my work for very long. I

need to stay focused on my tests, you understand, right?" He's getting good at this, so convincing.

Alex sighs and turns to Wiley. "I guess it's me and you."

"Oh, c'mon now, we make a great team. We're like Smokey and the Bandit, or... I don't know, some other awesome duo." Wiley smacks Alex on the back. "We can come up with nicknames, too." He's playing his part well.

Shaking his head, he grumbles, "No, no nicknames. Go get your things and we'll head out." He mutters, "This should be fun."

"Thanks, Alex. I think it'll be really beneficial to have that sample," Dad gushes. "If I can run the data of the sample against what we already have, it will help me categorize and isolate the common variables which will help me figure out what we're working with here."

Wiley exits the room, and a few moments later, Quinn and I leave, hopefully not making it quite so obvious we were all leaving at the same time.

We all meet in my bedroom, crammed in the far corner like sardines.

Wiley speaks quietly. "What's going on?"

Quinn says in a rush, "We have a theory, a procedure we want to run with Max and Skylar, but we need Alex out of the house. We don't want him to know anything until we know something totally concrete. Keith doesn't fully trust him."

"That makes sense why you've been all chipper today." He elbows me with a smirk.

"We really do need that sample," she adds. "But we also pushed the issue to get him out of the house."

"How long do you need?" Wiley asks.

"The good part of the day, at least. We'd like twenty-four hours, but we know that's probably not likely."

Shaking his head and soaking up the information, Wiley seeks approval, "Max, I can trust you, with Skylar, right?"

"Absolutely," I say honestly.

He hugs me and squeezes me tight, slapping me on the back. "Keep her safe. Keep yourself safe."

I hate that this feels like some type of goodbye.

"Here." Quinn hands him her backpack. "I put the supplies you two will need to get a sample. No clue how you'll pull it off, but I'm sure Alex will come up with something."

Only a few incredibly nerve-racking minutes go by before they're out the door and on their adventure. Dad, Quinn, and I stand on the porch and wave them goodbye until they're out of sight. When we can no longer see them, we make our way hurriedly into the house.

Dad clasps his hand onto my shoulder. "You ready?"

For a split second, I think about his question, *am I ready?* Am I ready for facing the things that terrify me headfirst? Am I ready for needles and being poked and prodded and the blood drained out of me and pumped into me and the unknown of whether or not this will work or if it will cause harm to either of us? Am I ready to do something after what seems like forever of doing nothing to try to bring Skylar back?

"Yeah, I'm ready," I say, totally terrified but totally willing to do what it takes.

28

———

MAX

"This will only pinch a little," Quinn proclaims, piercing my skin with a needle.

I'm unable to look away, even though the simple idea of what we're doing sends shivers down my spine and curdles my insides. My eyes close, and I try to imagine my happy place. I struggle to think of a time where I could escape, so I invent a new one. A place far away from here, or maybe right here, but with completely different circumstances.

The cabin but without the apocalypse, without the loss and destruction and constant deceit. Without the girl I'm falling head over heels for fighting to stay away from death's door. A place where we're safe, really, truly safe.

"You okay?" Quinn asks.

My eyes open slowly, and I find myself not wanting to leave my happy place. "Yeah."

"This gauge should allow for less pressure and more blood flow," Dad says to Quinn.

"Mmhm," she agrees. "And if I'm remembering correctly,

ten units should take around twenty-four hours, but given Skylar's weight, I'm assuming she's around six or seven units."

"Given she requires the full amount," Dad adds.

"Exactly, but that's what I don't really know. Plus, there's a limit to how much blood you can expel, but given they're also receiving, it makes things a little bit harder to figure out. Hemoglobin counts will take some time to recover, too."

My stomach gurgles. "Could I maybe have my headphones?"

"Don't be a baby," Quinn jokes.

"I could totally pass out if that makes things easier," I tease.

"Fine, fine, where are they?"

I point to the nightstand, and she snags them with her pinky and gives them to me. I use my free arm to grab the phone out of my pocket and awkwardly plug the headphones in. A few clicks and swipes later, I find some music that will help me drown out the mildly nauseating conversation Dad and Quinn are having.

"You done with that arm now?" Quinn asks.

"Yep," I reply.

Repeating the same steps, I extend it to her and close my eyes.

I tense momentarily and then relax semi-comfortably into the chair that they have situated slightly elevated from Skylar's position. Something about blood flow.

Despite my music, I overhear little bits of Quinn and Dad talking to each other but do my best to censor it out. I catch the words *central catheter* and *blood volume* but don't get enough of the rest to know what they were referring to. I know I should be more involved, listen and pay attention and learn, but honestly, I'm panicking. I've never been good with needles or blood or medical procedures and I can't allow my irrational fears to get in the way of this happening. It's best for all of us if I just distract myself.

Focus on my happy place. Focus on this all being over soon, but not in a *we're all going to die* kind of way, a *this is going to work, and we'll all be okay* kind of way.

A wave crashes over me, from head to toe, a sudden coldness followed by a massive surge of heat. My heart speeds up its pace, and I can't seem to figure out if it's because of the procedure or my lack of manliness in this situation. I struggle to control the panic forming in every grain of my body.

Keep it together, Max. Don't be a wuss. You can do this. It's only a little blood.

I recall Skylar's anxiety, how she stilled herself by breathing deeply through her nose and out through her mouth. I follow along, doing the same actions until I've calmed myself slightly.

A small, warm hand touches my upper arm. "You okay?" Quinn asks, looking concerned.

I force a smile and nod, shutting out the ever-growing queasiness wanting to take root, not wanting to tell her how I really feel. I know it's just the weirdness I have with this kind of stuff making me feel this way.

My gaze lingers down to Skylar, trailing the new IV line, matching the two that I have. The strand of hair that keeps falling in her face has managed to make its way onto her cheek. I ache to sweep it away but am rooted in place.

"How long until we know if it works?" I say into the room, hoping someone will answer.

Dad discloses, "Not sure. Can't say we've ever dealt with this sort of thing before."

"Okay," I say, unsure of how loud I'm talking because of having headphones on.

Dad looks my way, and with his deep-brown eyes carving

into me, he says, "You tell me if you start feeling any type of way, okay? I know you're freaking out a little, but you need to communicate if something is wrong."

"Okay," I lie.

I should tell him the truth, but I know if I do, he'll immediately pull the whole operation, and we'll be back to square one. Skylar can't afford to return to the drawing board. No matter what, we follow through on this. My blood has been the first and only solution that has given an insight into saving her. I knew there would be risks and I accepted them. No matter what happens to me, Skylar has to make it out of this.

29

WILEY

I am definitely not the guy for this job.

The diversion, yes, but the rest of what I've managed to sign myself up for, no.

This probably wasn't what Alex had in mind either. Hell, I wouldn't be surprised if he'd rather go alone than have me tag along.

It's not that I *mean* to be such a screw-up, it just happens naturally. The universe loves to troll me and somehow thinks making me trip over my own two feet is hilarious. Which, I can't blame it, it really is. I just think the ability to walk and chew gum should come effortlessly, not be a thing you constantly have to work on.

And maybe I'm exaggerating. Maybe I'm only being hard on myself because everyone around me is magically so damn useful.

Alex is a freaking superhero. The man can pretty much kick ass with whatever is thrown at him. He's smart and super capable.

Quinn is incredibly intelligent, soft-spoken but somehow

able to stand her ground and have brilliant ideas. Not to mention she's compassionate and massively selfless. Everything she's gone through and she still finds it in herself to help us.

Max is, well, Max. Completely irrational at times but one of the kindest and most thoughtful people I've encountered. Not to mention, if his blood saves my precious niece, Skylar, he wins at being the most useful of us all. Plus, have you seen him?

Don't even get me started on Keith. He somehow has the characteristics of every person in this group. Genius is the best word to sum him up.

Even in a partial coma, Skylar provides the ability to keep the group together, eyes on the task at hand. She's strong and brave, and I feel it in the deepest part of my soul that she will somehow make it out of this mess.

That leaves us with me. Good ol' Wiley. Means well but manages to screw up everything. At least I can be the comedic relief. I do best just hanging back, helping where I can. Doing what I'm told but never really coming up with the plans myself.

This leads me to how I got here, sitting in this SUV next to Alex, on our way to God knows where to find a blood sample of a mind-controlled psychopath.

To say it gives me a tiny post-traumatic stress is a bit of an understatement. It's not like I was captured, held against my will, and tortured by the very specific type of person we're looking to find. But I can't let myself succumb to that, because then I won't be of any use to the group I am trying so desperately to fit in with, to help. This group is my family, and I will do what it takes to play my part.

I rub the spot around my wrists where not too long ago I was zip-tied to a chair and beaten for information. We make our way toward our destination and my eyes flicker to the window, trees zooming along one by one.

Alex exhales. "You ready for this?"

"Yep," I gush happily. "What's the plan?"

"If I'm not mistaken, I know where a group should be. Small operation, we should be in an out pretty quickly."

Shit. We can't afford quickly, I'm supposed to stall him, at least for the day.

"Shouldn't we take our time? You know, do surveillance like they do in the movies and stuff?"

Alex laughs. "You think we're going to just sit in here, eat snacks and watch videos on our phones?"

I shrug. "Doesn't sound like the worst idea."

"Do you know what's going on?" he asks.

His question is so sudden and abrupt I don't even fully understand.

"What?" I say, dumbfounded.

"Back at the cabin, everyone is acting weird. Do you know what's going on?"

"Well, I don't know if you've noticed, but it seems there is some kind of apocalypse going on around us," I say lightly, hoping it throws him off.

"Always you with the jokes."

"What do you expect?" I laugh.

"Really, though," he says, clearly not wanting to let the question go just yet.

"I don't know, man. Everyone is freaking out about Skylar, for obvious reasons. She's important to us all. I think we're all a bit on edge," I say seriously, fingers crossed that maybe *this* will get him to leave it alone.

"Yeah, maybe. It's conveniently strange that Keith was keeping me in the loop and then all of a sudden had no more progress to tell me about."

"That's Keith for ya, though." Why won't he leave this alone?

"If you know something, you can tell me. I know they don't

take you as seriously as you'd like, but I can help you if you have information."

He's pushing hard, trying to get me to say something, to get me to crack. He's using some strange psychological manipulation to pit me against them. Too bad for him that I'm not that stupid; I won't fall for his tricks.

"Whoa now, you're overthinking things. What do you think is happening at the cabin?"

"I can't be certain, but I think there's been progress made. *Real* progress."

The way he verbalizes it sends chills through me. How does he know things by *not* knowing things? I know he's savvy at reading between the lines, but how is he able to read them this well?

"I think they'd probably tell me if there was progress. Skylar is my niece." I try not to be argumentative even though I'm lying my ass off.

"Unless you're hiding it from me, too."

He says the words, and they burn into me, searing my skin and seeping into my bones. I dislike having to keep things from him, but if Keith doesn't trust Alex with this information, then I shouldn't either. I have to stick with the plan. Play the oblivious minion just doing what they're told.

I laugh out loud, playing my part as best as possible when I say, "I'm a terrible liar."

30

———

MAX

Something doesn't feel right. *I* don't feel right.

Hot and cold take turns washing over me, and the nausea from before we began hasn't managed to subside. I want to say something; I *should* say something, but I can't.

Moments ago, in between the songs playing through my headphones, I overheard Quinn tell Dad that Skylar's vitals had improved.

I can't wimp out now.

I have to hold on a little longer. Each step into agony is one step closer to saving Skylar.

Dad pops one of my earbuds out and asks, "You doing okay, champ?"

I swallow hard and nod, silently fighting the urge to vomit.

"You don't look so good, are you sure?"

I have to put on a better show, make them believe that I'm doing better than I am.

"Yeah, I'm good." I change the subject. "How are things going?"

"We've managed to transfuse around two units, maybe more."

I have no idea what that means, nor do I know how to apply it to how things are going.

"Layman's, Dad."

"Right, sorry. I'd say we're near the halfway point, and we're making great progress. Skylar's vitals are much more stable. Even so much as the color is returning to her cheeks."

It's then that I allow my gaze to wander to her face for the first time since we started. I've been so terrified something would go wrong that I've forced myself into solitude this entire time. He's right, though, the color really has come back, not fully, but enough to make a drastic difference in the paleness from only a few hours ago. Her cheeks radiate a flushness I have ached to see in the last couple of weeks.

Oh, how I have missed her. Longed for her to be here, to be alive and well, and safe. And maybe, just maybe, she will be. Maybe this might actually work. Skylar and I have an intense history, and I have always felt a power, something unknown but brilliantly massive, pulling us together. I know how crazy and foolish that sounds, but I can't help but feel like we were meant to be on this path called life jointly. The idea of living in a world without Skylar is unnerving and hopelessly void. But perhaps the reason we were on this journey wasn't for us to *be* together, but for me to save her, to rescue her from this anguish.

Knowing that I could be the person to save her, to sacrifice myself for her, that alone will be the idea I cling so desperately to as I fall deeper and deeper into this abyss, this darkness consuming me from the inside. With every ounce of her blood that enters my body, I feel heavier and further detached from reality.

"You still with me, buddy?" Dad confirms.

When I bring my eyes from Skylar's delicate face to his, I see the worry lining his brow.

"She really does look better, doesn't she?" I say, sounding hopeful.

Quinn appears in my line of sight. "Absolutely, even better than anticipated." She hesitates for a second and continues. "Well, obviously we've only been speculating, this is foreign to us all."

"What's next?" I ask while maintaining my façade.

Quinn responds. "We've done nearly all we can do at this point. Now we just continue to monitor every single little thing we can until we have a bigger breakthrough."

Dad adds, "Like I said, we're about halfway through what we are expecting to transfuse, which is a massive transfusion for both of you. We have to play it safe and pay attention to any side effect or issue that may arise."

"Speaking of which," Quinn chimes in. "Here, put this under your tongue for a minute." She waves a thermometer in front of my face.

It takes me longer than I want for my brain to tell my mouth to open. The sluggishness settles into me cripplingly.

Quinn frowns. "Close your mouth."

The glass is cold at first, sending pricks of chilliness through my body, but then melts into the warmness of my mouth. An infinity passes, and she removes the now blistering hot thermometer.

This time its Dad who frowns, looking over Quinn's shoulder to see the temperature.

"Is that one hundred something?" he asks.

"Yeah, but it's okay."

He raises his voice slightly. "What do you mean *it's okay?* He has a fever."

"It would be more worrisome if he *didn't* have a fever. The fever means his body is doing what it's supposed to be doing, fighting the virus that we're essentially injecting him with."

Realizing that he overreacted, he quietly says, "Oh, right." His shoulders relax with each word.

"Granted, he looks like crap. There aren't any other symptoms present, which is a really good thing, considering," Quinn adds with confidence.

If only they knew.

My body feels like it's being dipped into Hell and then thrown into a blizzard, alternating between the two and forcing my mind to blur into a massive puddle of incoherence. My heart aches with the thought that this is what Skylar has been experiencing these last couple weeks. Has she been battling this same hell on earth? I would go through this a million times over if it meant pulling her from this nightmare.

"You want to grab him some ice water?" Quinn asks Dad.

"Okay." He lingers and then quickly strides out of the room.

Quinn leans down closer and speaks in a hushed voice, "You sure you're okay?" Her eyes are pleading. "You can tell me."

Now is my opportunity. I can trust Quinn. I know she would understand; understand the sacrifice I'm making for the girl I love. Understand that I would go through hellfire to save Skylar from an ounce of pain and anguish. If I tell her, maybe she can figure something out, figure out why I'm being dragged under and how to fix it, disallowing something worse to happen. Before I'm drawn too far and can't fight my way back out.

But what if I'm wrong, what if she pulls the IVs, the whole incredibly risky experiment, or worse, she tells my dad and he completely disregards my blood being of any use.

I can't let that happen so I do the only thing I can.

Maybe I'm foolish.

Maybe this is the wrong decision.

But there's always the possibility that maybe this is the right thing to do.

The thing that I have to do.

I shake my head and say, "I'm okay," and force a smile.

———

31

QUINN

I know Max is lying.

But I also know how much he cares for Skylar, and how important she is, not only to him but the people around us. So, it only makes sense that he would lie, pretend he's fine when *something* is clearly wrong. I just don't know the extent to which that *something* is wrong.

He could easily feel like crap, which would make sense, considering the *known to be dangerous virus* we are injecting in him. Or, he could be falling ill to said virus and succumbing to the same outcome that Skylar once did.

If it wasn't for Skylar's condition improving drastically, I would call off the procedure. If we can even call this a procedure. Keith and I don't even *really* know what we're doing. But somehow, we're managing. Somehow, we seem to be well over the halfway point and making progress. Literal life-changing progress.

I can only hope that it's life-changing for the positive.

If I were in Max's shoes, I would do the same; I would go through any amount of torment to save Cynthia, liberate her from the demonic state she was in. But I know I can't. There is no amount of wishing on shooting stars to turn back the clocks and save her. I can only do what I can to move forward and help Max and Skylar in this moment. And that's why I'll hold out a little longer, I'll push on and keep monitoring Max's vitals and do what I can to keep him teetering on this all-consuming edge.

He's closed his eyes again, and although I can only assume it brings him comfort, it freaks me out that the virus has taken him under. The more color that presents itself in Skylar is the less color I find in Max.

Her breathing has become more consistent, her blood pressure and pulse have improved, even her body temperature seems to be normalizing itself. I'm not one to jump ahead of myself, but there is a great possibility that we might be able to pull this off. I carefully remove the nasogastric feeding tube from Skylar, partly because it's nearly time to change, and because I'm hopeful it won't be needed much longer.

Each second ticks by, and I wonder how much more time we have before Wiley and Alex return to the cabin. They're bound to arrive at some point unless something horrible happens. I want them both back in one piece, safely, but I can't help wanting more time. I haven't even considered what will happen when they do arrive. Will we be able to keep Alex out of here? Keep him from knowing what we've been doing and provide him with some type of update to suffice him in the meantime?

Keith and I should really start figuring that out.

"Hey," I speak, studying his face.

His eyebrows do this scrunchie thing they always seem to do when he's spilling his brain onto a piece of paper.

"Just jotting down these last few notes," he says gradually, careful not to break his own concentration. With a click of his pen, he finishes and gives me his attention. "What's up?"

"What's the plan for when the guys get back?" I ask expectantly, trusting that maybe he's already come up with a plan.

"Good question," he offers, scratching his chin. "I knew the inevitable was coming, just haven't put too much thought into it."

"You could tell them I need some time alone with Skylar." The voice cracks as weakness sinks its teeth into him.

I turn to see Max's eyes slowly opening, his heavy head lifting itself off of his chair.

"Tell them I'm upset or something, not handling things well, and I need some time."

My heart breaks for him, not really knowing the pain he's putting himself through, but knowing his love is so strong he would do anything for her.

"That could work," Keith declares. "But I'll have to have some sort of update, some kind of progress from the day. Alex is suspicious already."

"You could just tell him you haven't made any. That you've been at a standstill without the mind-controlled blood sample. That you'll get update him once you analyze the sample." I pause and then say the thing that no one wants to consider, "Given they make it back." I immediately regret the words but know I can do nothing to erase them from existence. My attention wanders to the floor and sticks like glue, tracing the pattern of the butterscotch hardwood.

A noise startles me from my self-induced distraction, something close to a whimper.

I look to Keith and then immediately to Max, who is completely unfazed and has his eyes closed again, totally weirding me out.

It's then that I consider the alternative, shifting my focus to Skylar.

I rush closer, grabbing Keith's arm in anticipation as I approach. Her lip quivers, eyes flashing rapidly against her eyelids, flicking her luscious lashes.

"Max," I say without removing my eyes from her. I don't hear a peep, so I repeat myself, only louder this time, "Max."

He grunts and opens his eyes, responding with, "What is going on?" A certain clarity, strength, and urgency return to his voice.

"Just, just... I don't know," I manage to reply.

"It can't be," Keith whispers to himself.

I grab Skylar's wrist and immediately check her pulse, counting a steadier-than-ever heartbeat. I nearly jump out of my skin when her fingers tense slightly as I go to set her hand down.

Just then, her eyes flutter open, and she sucks in a breath. I find myself in complete disbelief that we did this, we brought her back. Somehow, despite having the odds stacked against us, we did the impossible.

In the smallest whisper, Max says, "Skylar."

And when I turn to him, a single tear falls down his pale cheek.

32

———

MAX

The world has stopped spinning. My heart, seemingly motion-less and in utter shock. And then, rushing together all at once, I breathe and suck in a blissfully gaping lungful of life, for seeing Skylar, awake, has been like a defibrillator to the chest.

A million emotions rush through me.

Complete and utter gratitude, a welcoming euphoria purely from seeing her vivid eyes blink into existence.

Her dry and chapped lips part to speak, but she can't seem to find the words or her voice. Her eyes, now lined with tears, frantically scouring the room, from person to person.

Quinn finally does the thing we all seem to be struggling with. Her voice small and comforting, she says, "Skylar, every-thing is okay. Everything is going to be okay."

The burrow of Skylar's brow seems to show no relief from Quinn's words.

I start to speak but stumble on the lump that's formed in my throat. Skylar's gaze settles on me, looking me up and down, studying the things attached to my body, and then her gaze falls to her sides, at the contraptions attached to her.

"W-what's happ-happening?" she manages.

Her voice like paradise to my ears, despite the gaspiness. Oh, how I have dreamed of the day when I would hear her speak again, even if it was *Max, go away*, just to hear her sweet voice would mean that she was okay.

A tear rolls its way down my cheek, and I dig down to find my strength to pull it together. I can't make it this far to lose my shit here, not now.

"You're going to be okay," I declare, offering what I can of a smile, pain blistering from my insides, the darkness dragging me under.

She peers from her sides and then to me. "Are you?"

Her words pierce like sharp knives. Somehow, despite the hell she's been through, she's asking about *me*. A laugh bubbles up out of my chest, hysteria taking hold.

I begin to stand, to move closer to Skylar, but a hand on my shoulder pushes me into my seat. Struggling to get my eyes to focus, I attempt to swat away the resister, managing to pull at the IV in my arm, sending shocks of pain through me.

"Max, you need to sit still, you know you can't get up right now," Quinn's commands.

I still can't seem to see her distinctly. Blinking excessively, I wipe at my eyes, trying to rid the murkiness that has formed.

"I... I can't see," I say in a rush, mourning the words once they come out. I can't say things like this. I can't let them know anything is wrong. Just because Skylar is awake and coherent, doesn't mean she's in the clear. Who's to say if we stop now, that she wouldn't revert back to how she was. I can't afford to let that happen, not after all of this.

Dad and Quinn are at my sides in a flash, hovering and murmuring words to each other that I can't seem to make out. Through the mush of it all, one of them says, "We have to stop."

Words shape and bubble out of my mouth, "No, no, we, no..."

Frantically, I find myself looking in what I think is the direction of Skylar as I catch the sweet sound of her voice, "What's wrong? What's happening? Why won't you tell me what's going on?"

It's so strange that her voice is crystal clear like she's some angel sent down from Heaven to greet me.

"Please, we can't stop, I'll be fine," I command myself to say and simultaneously will myself to pull it together. Despite the fear creeping in, consuming me fully, I resist the urge to let it do its job. I remember reading once, or maybe I saw it on a show, that great things are on the other side of fear, the best things in life even. I have to believe that this is true for right now, greatness will come from this.

"Temporary vision loss could be a blood flow issue," Quinn advises.

I scan the room to try to locate her body.

"Are you in any pain?" she says, an outline of her small figure appearing beside me, her too-warm hand on my wrist, finding my pulse.

I shake my head, lying because I know damn well I can't tell them the truth right now. Not until I know Skylar is fine.

A loud thud startles me, followed by Dad saying, "What the hell was that?"

I panic, not being able to see clearly, almost like the lights have been turned way down and the autofocus on the room has completely been shut off.

I shift all of my effort to my hearing—straining. I'm able to make out what resembles footsteps.

Shit.

Either Wiley and Alex have returned or something worse has happened, someone has found us. Considering we're pretty well hidden, and not many people know we even have a place out here in the deepest part of these thick woods, I have to assume the former. At this moment, neither option is appealing.

A deep, undoubtedly angry voice breaks into the room, "What the hell is going on in here?"

And then a rush of wind passes me followed by Wiley's voice, "Oh god, Skylar. Skylar, is that you?"

"Who else would it be?" Her humor intact despite everything.

"I can't believe this," he says, his voice trembling.

"Neither can I. I can't believe you're okay. I thought I'd never see you again."

"Nothing can hold back ol' Wiley," he jokes.

"Someone had better tell me what's going on," Alex orders.

So much for the cover-up, the potentially dangerous distraction we talked Wiley into tagging along on. How much time has passed? What time even is it? Were they able to get the blood sample?

Question after question overflow my thoughts and distract me from the only question I can't be bothered to ask: *Am I going to be okay?*

33

SKYLAR

Time ticked by, and I struggled with the realization that I might never make it out of the darkness. All things terrible—fear, pain, weakness, sadness, hopelessness—consumed every last bit of me until there was nothing left. There were fleeting moments of relief when I heard him speak; it was like a bright shining light was breaking through the forever endless depths of my despair.

Telling me to hold on.

That I was loved.

That he needed me.

That he would save me.

I held on to those words, those brief seconds of reprieve each time I fell deeply under. I fought every desire to give up in hopes that he was right. There were moments I'd never wanted to give up more in my life, the pain coursing through my body and the battle I fought inside my head, reliving past traumas I had long since pushed out. I convinced myself I wasn't strong enough to handle the torment but when I was hanging on barely by a thread, his voice sang like a sweet melody, telling me to hold on a little longer.

The rawness, the ache and need filling his voice as he pulled me from the brink of the end, kept me going when nothing else could.

I needed him just as much as he needed me, and there was a calming comfort in the simple yet complete complexity.

And now, even gazing at his pale but somehow still beautiful face, I know he needs me more than ever. Whatever is happening, whatever he did to bring me back, is now pulling him under, and I can't let that happen.

"These," I say, shifting my focus to the IVs attached to my arms. "Take them off."

Quinn shakes her head.

Who the hell put her in charge?

Max speaks. "No, I'm fine. We have to finish."

"Finish what?" I say frantically.

The angry man, I think his name is Allen, reiterates, "Finish what? Someone needs to start explaining, now," with a heavy emphasis on the last word.

Why are they being so secretive? Who is this mystery Allen guy, and why does he look so familiar? Why can't they stop whatever they're doing?

Keith grabs Allen's arm and leads him to the door. "Alex, a word in private."

Ohh, Alex, not Allen.

Quinn moves toward me, reaching for my wrist. I flinch and pull away, not understanding why she's touching me.

"Skylar." Max's voice smooth like honey, "you can trust Quinn."

I eye her, and she offers a shy smile.

"I'm here to help," she adds.

"Help with what?" I say, extending my arm to her.

She gently turns it upward, placing her two fingers to find my pulse.

Wiley chimes in. "Quinn here is a whiz at medical stuff. She's been caring for you since *the accident*. Well, Max and Keith have, too, but Quinn has done the brunt of the work."

When he says *the accident,* my mind races around in a panic to remember what he means.

"The accident?" I say slowly, not understanding.

"What's the last thing you remember?" Quinn asks.

I allow my thoughts to run wild, bouncing around trying to make sense and create a timeline.

"I remember Max," I say gently, my eyes wandering to meet his.

"You remember him carrying you?" She adds the words like she's helping to put the pieces together for me.

"What? No," I say, unsure of what she's insinuating. "I remember him talking to me...telling me to hold on." The memory floods in, pulling at my heartstrings. The desperation in his voice telling me to come back to him.

"You-you heard me?"

"Was that real?" I ask, pleading I didn't just create that in my subconscious.

"Yeah," he says, tears lining his emerald eyes.

"What about prior to that?" Quinn interrupts.

"Just tell me, please. This is painful." And although painful is a massive overexaggeration compared to what I've been through, this whole guessing game is wasting time.

"There was a situation in the water. We had to cross a creek bed, and you went under. Max was able to pull you out, but before we got to the cabin you fell into a comatose condition. We've been working pretty much nonstop to figure out how and why and do everything we could to prolong your life. It wasn't until Max's blood proved vital to your progress that there was any hope. Max is essentially filtering your blood through him and pumping you full of clean blood."

She stops speaking, and a ton of bricks hit me as I process the information.

"You have to stop." I feverishly look from Max to Quinn in a panic. "You can't do this to him."

"No, a little longer," Max begs. "I have to know you're okay."

"I'm okay," I say, fighting the tears that are welling uncontrollably. "I'm okay and I'm here, just please, please stop. I don't need any more."

He smiles sweetly, paleness consuming him and sweat forming on his brow.

I take it back; I take it all back. I would return to my eternal hell if it meant not letting him suffer through any of this.

I can't lose him, not after losing him over and over in the past. He's too important, he always has been. Max was my first best friend, the only person I ever truly trusted and cared for. The only person who saw me as I was and still wanted to be around. I pushed him away and I regret every bit of it. I was wrong when I thought I was doing the right thing by not letting him in. He made a promise to protect me, but who is going to protect him? Our paths have been intertwined from the start, and I can't let this sickness take him away.

34

MAX

Alex's voice carries into the room. "You could have *told* me. Did you even need the blood sample?"

"Yes," Dad says calmly. "I really do. There's still so much I have yet to figure out."

Alex exhales loudly before saying, "Okay."

"Okay, then," Dad adds, seeming a bit surprised.

One set of footsteps follow the other into the room.

Alex asks, "So, fill me in on what's going on."

Skylar claims. "We can stop now, I'm fine. I'm alive and well and all that." Her voice is still weak but such a pleasant gift to my ears.

"I think it's best if we wait just a little longer," Quinn claims.

"If someone doesn't take these IVs out, I'm going to do it myself," Skylar insists as she grows adorably furious.

"Keith, can you check your numbers, see where we're at?" Quinn asks impatiently.

"What can I do?" Wiley questions, looking from person to person.

The blur of him shifting to and from in my line of sight.

"I could use some water," Skylar says because no one seems to accept Wiley's help.

A scorching wave of heat takes its turn punishing me, forcing me to wince. Bile rises into the back of my throat, and I swallow it down at the last second.

"That's it." Skylar yelps. "I'm done." She places her right hand against her left arm, where the IV is placed, and dead stares at Quinn. "Now is your last chance. Either you do it or I will."

"Give me a second, hold on, just one second, Sky," Dad advises.

"I'm done waiting. You guys are killing him, how do you not see that?" She's angry.

I have to show her that I'm fine.

"I'm okay," I mutter and fight down another bout of bile that forces its way up.

"Go ahead, Quinn. We're right on the edge but we should be okay."

"No," I say. I can't do the edge; I need to know we're far enough. "Please, a little m-more," I stutter. What is happening to me? I'm so...weak...and disoriented. I imagine this is what it's like to be drunk, but instead of booze, I'm drunk on death.

A rush of noises fills the room. Shuffling of feet. Unhooking of equipment. Whispers and commands. The room spins like I'm being sucked up into a vacuum, swirled around violently, then thrown out into space with no life support. My head shrinks, and my skin is pulled apart, melted and frozen at the same time. My insides crushed and shaken.

Then hands.

Small and warm and perfect and delicate hands.

All I can concentrate on is the hands.

The hands attached to the soul I fought so desperately to save.

"Max," she breathes and places a hand against my cheek. It burns but in such a heavenly way. "What have you done, you silly boy?"

I blink profusely, trying to clear my vision, and when I do, I notice the tears rolling down her face. I ache to take her suffering away. I don't want her to cry. I did this for her. She has to know this.

"I...missed you," I admit, and it's so pathetic and lame and probably the worst thing to say right now, but it's what comes out.

She smiles and tears overflow from her sky-deep eyes. My hand finds its way to her face, and I graze my knuckles along her skin before tucking that ever-persistent strand of hair behind her ear. Her eyes close, and she leans into my hand, taking hers and pressing them both against her cheek. Happiness floods me momentarily, followed by another surge of agony. I flinch and she gasps, removing her hand and standing abruptly.

"Do something," she orders.

"All right, Max, you have to talk to me," Quinn instructs. "Tell me what you're feeling." She greets me like I'm a child who has just told their mother they didn't feel well.

I imagine her asking me what hurts, and I find myself unable to pinpoint the pain. My arms, my legs, my head, all of my insides, even my skin hurts.

"Everything," I manage to say, although I know it's of no help. I don't know how to describe what I'm feeling.

"Are you in pain?" she asks, doctorly.

"Y-yes."

"Where?"

"Everywhere."

Skylar speaks, but not to me. She's facing Quinn and Dad now, or at least that's what the blur in my vision appears to be doing. "You can give him something, right? Pain medicine at least?"

"I was hoping to avoid treating him with anything that has fever-reducing capabilities. We need his fever to fight the virus."

"That's garbage, right, Keith? You can give him something, can't you? He's in *pain*. How can you do this to him?"

"What about a sedative?" Wiley offers, somehow sounding both clueless and supportive.

"That's not a terrible idea," Dad says, considering the option.

Quinn adds, "We could do something very short term. Something to take the edge off and let him rest."

"And what happens if he doesn't wake up?" Skylar warns. "What happens if you've just transferred what was wrong with me to him?"

"Well, I mean, we have," Quinn asserts. "But Max's body can process and eliminate the virus, so in theory, he should cleanse himself."

"In theory? Are you serious right now?" Skylar barks.

"You're telling me that Max is the cure to the virus?" Alex questions.

Dad's silhouette shifts in my line of sight, facing the sound of Alex. "No, not technically. He has no impact on the deranged, only the comatose." He hesitates and then adds, "I still need to run tests against the mind-controlled, but otherwise, this seems like an isolated and short-lived line of progression."

Exhaustion settles over my body, slowing down the words and movements of those around me. My eyes close on their own free will, and I struggle to sit upright.

"Can we move him? At least get him more comfortable?" Skylar grabs under my arm and tries her best to hoist me up, but my body sags, and she makes no advance. "A little help, please?" Her voice strains, and her efforts continue to get us nowhere.

A stronger set of hands approach, and a few seconds later I'm transported from the chair I've called home the last couple weeks to the bed where I pleaded to Skylar night after night. My weight settles heavily into the mattress, relieved to be horizontal.

"Should I cover him, should I not? What am I supposed to do?" Skylar asks someone, probably Quinn.

"Max," Quinn's boasts, her voice multiple notches above what it should be. "Are you hot or cold?"

"Yes."

She laughs slightly, and it's inappropriate and out of place, but I can't help but smile, too.

"Blanket it is," she tells Skylar.

"I'm going to, uh, clean up. Let me know if I can be of any help," Wiley reveals uncomfortably. "You," he says, resulting in me opening my eyes and straining to see who he's talking to, "need to rest. Just because you're awake doesn't mean you need to be running around here trying to lift boys and stuff."

"Sinclair," Alex starts, "you and I will catch up soon. We need to figure out what to do with this information and how to move forward. *The Resistance* will be expecting us soon."

"You're crazy if you think we're going anywhere with you anytime soon," Quinn huffs.

"Right there with ya, girl," Skylar inserts.

"As I said, Keith, you and I will talk."

He leaves the room, his footsteps heavy. A moment passes, and there's a collective sigh followed by someone speaking.

"You okay, buddy?" Dad settles his weight onto the bed, sitting next to me.

"I've been better," I manage.

He wipes at my forehead with his hand. "Hey, Sky, grab me a tissue."

Seconds later, he blots my face. "You're going to get through this, okay?"

I nod my head as best as I can, trying my hardest to believe him.

I don't see how there is any coming back from this. This all-consuming darkness grabbing hold, sinking its teeth into every single inch of my body, sending failure codes and blowing all of the fuses.

"Okay," I say to appease him.

Skylar sits on the opposite side of the bed, the mattress giving way slightly beneath her. What I would give for both of us to be fine, away from this continuous shitstorm we keep facing.

She intertwines her fingers into mine, and I think that maybe dying like this wouldn't be the worst thing in the world.

Like she was reading my mind, Skylar says, "Don't go dying on me."

I crack what I can of a smile. "Morbid much?"

She sniffles and squeezes my hand gently.

Dad removes himself from the bed, and I study the shuffling of his feet as he makes his way toward Quinn. He speaks, but I can't seem to make out the words.

Skylar leans down closer and sighs, "I missed you, too, ya know?"

My heart thumps heavily, and with what last remaining ounce of strength I have, I say softly, "I need you," and everything fades to black.

35

SKYLAR

I'm not really sure how it's possible to be so full of love but yet so heartbroken at the same time. I press my lips to his forehead and feel part of myself slipping away with him.

Quinn's hands find their way to my shoulders. "Hey." She says the word so delicately like I'm this fragile thing that could break at any second.

She offers a considerate smile, and I forget why I initially ever disliked her.

"Do you mind if I check your vitals? I know you're worried about Max, but you've been through a lot, too."

"Sure." I reach for a tissue off the nightstand, settle into the recliner's seat and ask, "So, you're like a doctor or something?"

She snickers. "No, not really."

"Don't let her fool you," Keith presses, pulling my attention. "That girl's *real* smart." He points his long lanky finger at her. "She's the one who kept you alive when we weren't sure how to save you. Things would have been a lot worse without her."

I shift my eyes to study her, and my gaze settles over her

dark wavy hair and onto her bright blue-grey eyes. Her face portrays a softness, almost kind but somehow afraid and wounded like she's hiding some horrible secret.

She mumbles. "I know some basics."

"Basics?" He mocks her and chuckles before continuing. "You did a procedure that probably hasn't even ever been done, and you did it successfully."

He talks like he's known Quinn her whole life, and I can't tell whether that makes her uncomfortable or happy. She's humble, that's for sure.

"You two seem like old friends," I say, observant yet dubious.

"Keith is the genius here, not me. He's the one who even figured out that Max's blood could help you."

"I had a theory," Keith admits. "Max was the one who irrationally stuck you with a full syringe of his blood without telling any of us."

"No way," I say, not able to hide my surprise.

"He's been a mess without you," Quinn recalls. "If we told him he had to chop off both of his arms to save you, he would have done it in a heartbeat."

My own heart seems to beat twice as fast with her words, and I recall his pleas to come back to him, the only hope I was able to hold on to during those dark days. I allow my gaze to fall on him, pain ripping through me at seeing exactly what he's seen these last couple weeks—the person he cares for most, hanging on to life by a thread. His ashy locks are damp with sweat, falling limp across his forehead, stubble only barely forming, the arch of his jawline tense.

"How are you feeling?"

The question seems simple, but I find myself struggling to conjure words. How do I feel?

"Tired, I guess," I manage.

"Are you experiencing any pain, discomfort?" *Just in my heart.*

I avoid her question when I ask, "How long will he be like this?"

"Honestly," she says and then lets out a sigh. "I don't know. I hope not long. The sedative we gave him will hopefully get him through the night, allow for some time to rest so his body can fight the virus."

"And you're sure this will work?" I ask, not really sure if I want to know the answer.

"Nothing is certain, but we're counting on it."

"Have some faith, Sky," Keith suggests while continuing to tidy up the space.

"Do you want anything to eat?" Quinn asks.

"I'm not very hungry." How can I eat when Max is lying there lifeless like this? But then how can I allow myself to wither away when he sacrificed everything for me? "But I guess I could try something small."

"You really should get your strength up," Keith says. "We were artificially feeding you the last week or so. It might do your body good to get something solid in there."

Artificial feeding? What the hell happened to me? There's still so much I haven't pieced together. Like who the strange guy is who's mad at being out of the loop.

"Hey," I say in a hushed whisper. "Who's the guy? Alex?"

Quinn and Keith both stop their fidgeting to look at me

"He's the guy who saved Wiley. Rescued him and brought him to us."

"Really?"

"Yeah." He continues, "Do you remember that building we got supplies from, the one we stole the UTV from?"

I rack my brain, recalling the memories flooding in, one followed by another. The men came inside, and we had to hide behind those shelves. I had thought we were goners. Max had caught the weight of my body as I leaned against him, nearly passing out from fear. Then we were nearly caught again when Keith had to fix the wires from where Max had tried to hotwire the UTV. The men ran toward us but then just stood there like statues as we drove away in their prized possession. The pieces click into place, the men, that man, the one who got closest to us. The face, so distinct and familiar.

Perhaps seeing the pieces of the puzzle clicking together in my head, he confirms, "Alex was the man from the warehouse. Alexander Sanchez."

"Wow, that's insane," I say, almost inaudibly.

"You're telling me," Keith retorts. "The night they showed up, we were all ready to throw down. Talk about a relief hearing Wiley's voice through that door. Max and I nearly jumped each other to open the door."

I was so afraid I would never see Wiley again. The closest thing I have to a stable family ripped away by some freaks trying to kill us. Max held himself responsible for what happened to Wiley, and I know he would have gone to look for him at some point. We both would have, except for the whole *me sorta falling into a deep, dark coma* thing. I can only imagine the relief Max felt—the guilt that was lifted—when Wiley appeared out of nowhere.

I lower my voice quieter and lean in. "He said something about a *resistance?* What's he talking about?"

Keith scans the room, settles on Quinn, then Max, and then me. "It's a long story, a really, really, long story." He pauses for a second. "Short version is there's a *second* organized group, trying to fight against the *first* organized group who unleashed this virus. I guess that's what they call themselves *The Resistance.*"

"That's good then, right?" I say, not understanding the

apprehension lining his face.

He exhales heavily. "I just don't know if we can trust Alex."

36

SKYLAR

I doze on and off most of the night, never really feeling like I had fallen asleep. Stuck in the teeter-totter of the in-between. I dreamt of standing in front of the mirror, blonde hair down my shoulders, but at a closer look, I could see all of my teeth coming loose, one by one falling out. Another time, I dreamt Max was on a train and I was running next to it, desperate to latch on to his arm as he passed me by, each time failing. That dream seemed to play itself on repeat.

When I wasn't battling the terrors of my subconscious, I was staring at Max in the real world. Desperately watching his chest rise and fall with each breath, making sure he was still here. Twice through the night, Quinn drifted in to check on us, taking our pulse, blood pressure, and temperature. Both times she reassured me that Max would be okay and that I should get my rest, that I would need it.

"You hungry?" She strolls into the room carrying a tray full of what smells like heaven.

My stomach growls like it's trying to answer her itself.

"Yeah, thank you." I smile.

"Figured you would want to eat in here and not with the stinky boys." She puts the tray on the solid oak dresser, the first flat surface that's decently cleared off, and brings me a plate of heaping pancakes.

"Wow," I say in amazement. "This smells wonderful. Did you make these?"

She shakes her head. "Keith is a master pancake maker." Quinn takes a seat opposite me and then pauses. "I didn't ask. Do you mind?"

"What? No, of course not," I respond, embarrassed she had to ask. The first bite of pancake sends insane amounts of happiness through me, and I suddenly feel guilty Max isn't experiencing this, too.

"Good, thanks. I hate sitting out there with all of them. It's so weird, ya know?"

I don't know, actually.

"What do you mean?"

"Well, things are...strange. Alex is clearly impatient with everything that's going on, Keith seems stuck in his tunnel vision, which involves not really keeping Alex up to date, and Wiley...poor Wiley is like a fly on the wall, just waiting for his next order. And I mean that in the nicest way possible. Wiley is so quick to do whatever is asked of him, but Alex is Alex, and Keith is Keith, and it's just...very tense."

"So, like," I say between bites, "what's the plan?"

Quinn swallows the mound of food in her mouth. "Not sure, really. Alex seems to want us to leave, and Keith," she lowers her voice, "doesn't seem to be buying what he's selling."

"Yeah, Keith is a skeptic for sure," I say, matter-of-fact, holding on to a syrup-drenched pancake bite dangling from my fork. "What do you think?"

She shrugs. "I don't know. I barely know any of you, but I trust Keith and Max."

I instinctually cringe at the last word, but a lot less than I did when we first met. Maybe the fact that Max basically sacrificed himself for me makes me a bit more secure in how he feels about me.

"He should be awake soon, right?" Selfishly, I had been hopeful he would have already awoken, but I haven't wanted to rush any progress his body could make while he was asleep.

"Yeah." She hesitates and looks to the clock. "Sometime soon."

"I...um, I haven't properly thanked you," I say anxiously. "You know, for being here. For me, and for Max. I appreciate it more than you know."

Her cheeks redden slightly. "It's no problem."

"And I wanted to say I'm sorry."

Quinn's brows crinkle together. "What for?"

Where do I even start? I guess the beginning. "I didn't exactly give you the warmest welcome, and I'm sorry for that. We had one hell of a few days and we all so desperately wanted to be safe. I was stressed out and emotionally drained. Max and I had been at each other's throats the entire trip and...and he goes and jumps out of the truck to save this beautiful girl. I let my emotions get the best, or, well, worst of me." My eyes settle onto hers, red and rimmed with tears. "I'm sorry."

She smiles sheepishly. "You think I'm beautiful?"

I laugh. "Such a girl to be taking *that* from what I said."

At this, she laughs, and then we both giggle at each other like idiots.

A moment passes, and the laughter fizzles out like an old can of Coke.

"Just for the record, he's not exactly my type."

She must be crazy; Max is any girl's type. Tall but not lanky. Gorgeous brown locks falling over his to-die-for forest-green eyes. Plus, the not-so-superficial features, like his selflessness and big beautiful brain. He's the perfect mix of his parents —Keith's brilliance, and Maura's kindness. Don't get me wrong, he's also irrational and super dumb at times, but he means well and is one hell of a catch.

"That's impossible," I say in disbelief.

"Trust me," she offers with a wink, and like a switch is flipped, sadness consumes her. "I'm off the market anyway."

"Oh, no," I say, realizing we're totally gossiping like friends right now. "Bad breakup?"

"You could say that," she says painfully. Something bad happened, something really bad.

Not only can I see it, but I can feel her sorrow pouring out of her like an overflowing bucket.

"Do you want to talk about it?" I offer kindly. "You don't have to; I just know that sometimes it helps to process if you get it somewhere other than just inside."

A tear rolls down her slightly freckled cheek, and I ache for her, my heart breaking a little with her. "She died."

With those two words, so many things click into place.

Not being interested in Max.

Her sadness.

Her being alone.

I cross the room and hold out my arms to her. "I'm so sorry." I know it doesn't matter, the words are empty and hollow, but that and my friendship are all I can really offer her right this second. Her person has been taken from her, and she's had the will to carry on and save my life.

I owe her more than I will ever be able to repay.

37

———

KEITH

Taking a long sip of his coffee, Alex says, "We need to talk." The *Okayest Dad Ever* mug Max gave me for Christmas years ago is held firmly in his grasp.

I can't keep avoiding him no matter how much I try. *Go away.* I don't know what to tell him. *I don't trust you.* I'm running out of lies and ways to stall him. *What if you're part of the problem?* He seems to know a lot of information about both sides of this war, and he claims to be on the *good* side, but who's to say he really is. He saved Wiley, yes—he's proven useful to us, yes—but at what cost to him and his cause? He's hiding something, and although I don't know what it is, I can't help but distrust him in the meantime.

"What's up?" I say nonchalantly.

"I know you're avoiding me," he confirms. "Can we at least get on the same page?"

"Same page with what?" I say, although the whole pleading ignorance thing doesn't suit me well and he knows it.

"Okay, let's start with something easy. The blood sample, the mind-controlled. What did you find?"

"Well," I say, taking a sip of my own coffee. "There were similarities between the mind-controlled sample, and Wiley and my blood. So clearly there are different strains of this virus and they're somehow specific to people."

"That's useful." He nods. "And Max is still an outlier?"

I swallow hard, not wanting to admit that my son's blood does not match any of ours. That it has no connection other than the life-saving abilities it's shown with Skylar.

"Correct."

"Did you test it against the mind-controlled?" Annoyance and aggravation line his voice, like he's irritated that he's even having to follow up with these questions.

"Yes."

"And?"

"Shows no sign of improvement. Seems that this is an isolated incident."

At this moment, Wiley returns from an excessively long bathroom break. "Sorry, had something stuck in my tooth." He points to his mouth and sits at the small, square dining table.

I glance at Wiley, but otherwise, we both ignore his presence during our weird standoff of a conversation. Everything I've told Alex has been the truth. Max's blood really is an outlier, it really is somehow potently beneficial to Skylar's condition, and it really does not impact the other conditions whatsoever. It's almost like he wants me to create something that isn't there. Give him some kind of update that says *I figured it out.* But I can't. I have limited supplies and resources and I feel like I'm only being told half the story.

"We really need to plan our leave soon. *The Resistance* will be of more assistance in providing you a proper lab and proper help."

"I'm not going anywhere," I do my best to maintain my cool, even though I want to yell at him, tell him to get out of my house and never return. Thanks for your help, but see ya later.

Alex's jaw tenses, and for just a second, I think I see Wiley flinch in my peripheral.

"That's going to be an issue," he counters.

I point in the direction of Max's bedroom. "You realize my son is in there partially sedated, running a fever and housing the entire contents of Skylar's tainted blood supply in his veins. He's fighting for his life, and you want me to plan a little vacation to *The Resistance?*" I then point to Wiley. "Not to mention his niece is recovering from a whole-body blood transfusion after being barely held alive the last few weeks."

He cuts me off and raises a hand. "I understand."

"Do you?" I say mockingly. "Do you really? Because I don't think you understand that my family is *here*, right in this house. And I will *not* begin to even consider leaving this cabin until everyone is on two feet."

"We had a plan," Alex continues.

"I don't care about your plan, Alex. Not until I know my family is safe. Otherwise, what would be the point? You honestly expect me to just drop everything and leave with you? Listen, I'm incredibly appreciative of what you've done—saving Wiley and bringing him to the cabin, and the dangerous supply runs—but you expect me to trust you even though you're hiding something from us?"

Perhaps my words striking a nerve, his whole demeanor changes, confusion settling in. "Hiding something?"

I throw my arms in the air and exclaim, "Yeah. You know we're not stupid. I don't know why you can't tell us the whole story. You just conveniently know so much about *The Resistance* and *The Reformation?*" The words come out in a rush, and part of me is regretful, the other part glad I finally got it off of my chest.

"We did our research," he explains.

I narrow my eyes on him. "Research? You're claiming you know all of this based on research?"

"Listen, we're on the same side. Fighting against the bad guys. The guys who have taken things and *people* from us."

The way he says 'people' sends chills up my spine. What does he know about having people taken from him?

From the corner of my eye, Wiley catches my attention, furiously chewing on his nails. I make brief eye contact with him, and he shrugs, clearly impartial to what's going on around him.

"I get it," Wiley concurs. "You're not wrong by not throwing your trust around freely. And if what Alex is saying is true, he's not wrong for urging this process along."

"Then what?" I petition.

"Then, I don't know, but you're both not wrong. I don't think anyway," Wiley retorts.

I can't do this right now. I don't have the time. Max should have been awake already, and even though this whole thing is entirely interesting, the danger that I've put my son in is a bit more pressing.

Alex clears his throat. "I had brought Wiley with the intention of recovering you, Sinclair. If you're no longer of use to us, then I'll have to take my leave without you. I'll give you until forty-eight hours to make a decision, at which point I'll be leaving. I do hope you make the right choice."

Nothing like one hell of an ultimatum.

I won't be pressured into going with him just because he wants it. Unless Max and Skylar both make some miraculous recovery, there's no way they could handle the journey—at least not with the world the way it is now.

Calm and collected, Alex leaves the room.

Wiley's eyes widen as he points to the absence and chuckles, "This guy?"

A smile cracks its way to my face, something Wiley always seems to manage. Even if Alex leaves, at least I have my family. Max, Wiley, Skylar, and even the newest member, Quinn. That's all that really matters anymore, and if the world is going to crap, this is the place where we should be. We have plenty of rations, medical equipment, clean water, electricity. Without Alex, we will have one less stressor. One less bodyguard but one less person to feed.

"He knows too much," Wiley articulates.

He catches me off guard, and when I look to his face, I see that he's no longer speaking lightly.

It's then that I realize that that's not it, he would be one more person who knows about Max's blood, and how he's virtually the only thing known to help rid this virus. He would run straight into the arms of his group and blab to them about all of this. Max's blood, the transfusion, the entire setup I've spent many years of my life building and securing. They would most definitely come for us.

I can't let that happen.

I can't let Alex leave.

38

SKYLAR

"He should be awake now, right? You said by the morning, and now it's clearly afternoon." I say the words and try not to panic. Ever since I opened my eyes yesterday, I've been in this constant state of trying not to freak out. Looking over and seeing Max with IVs trailing from him and running into my own arms, I knew something terrible was happening. His pale face laced with sweat even though I was miraculously being brought back to life.

Quinn shifts uncomfortably, doing a terrible job at hiding her worry. "Yeah, he should. But it's possible he's only reacting to the sedative. His body is under a lot of stress."

"He's going to be okay, though?" I say it like a question, even though as the words come out, they're more like something I'm trying to will into the universe—if I just believe it hard enough, it will come true.

He can't be gone.

"I hope so." Quinn shrugs. "I'm going to go check in with Keith. I'll be back shortly."

She walks out of the room, head down, bursting at the

seams with sadness. I imagine she's feeling guilty for pushing, for prolonging this procedure when it was sucking the life out of him. The guilt heavy realizing his undoing is on her hands.

Once she's fully exited the room, I grab on to Max's clammy hand, pressing my lips against it and securing it firmly in my grasp.

"Hey," I say, feeling a bit foolish. "I don't know if you can hear me, but I want you to know I'm right here, and I'm not going anywhere." I take a breath. "When I was in this exact place, just days ago, the one thing that kept me going was you. There were moments I didn't think I could take any more pain, and right as I was about to give up completely, I would hear you. So, if this is in any way the same, and you can hear me, please don't give up. Not only for me, but for your dad and Quinn and Wiley, and most importantly, you. You have so much more life to live.

"Do you remember when we were—oh man, we had to have been like four and five—and we were playing tag out front and I tripped over my own two feet? Busted my face on that step, there was blood everywhere. You were so grossed out, and I couldn't stop crying. In hindsight, it really was funny, how freaked out you were by the gash on my face and how freaked out I was that I was going to die. But no matter how you felt, you wouldn't let go of me. You hugged me and told me everything was going to be okay and you never let go of my hand, even as your mom bandaged me up. Even at such a young age, I knew how special you were. I've been such an idiot." I sniffle back the tears. "I'm sorry, Max, I'm so sorry. For everything— for pushing you away, for all of the lost years—for this, for not being able to save you when all you ever do is save me.

"I don't deserve you, I never will, but I won't just accept you leaving us like this. Fight, Max. Please fight, come back to us."

Approaching footsteps startle me into reality.

"Sky," Keith announces, striding into the room. "How are you feeling?"

"Despite the circumstances, not bad."

"Any headaches, nausea, pain?"

"Nope, a quick shower and your pancakes seemed to do the trick."

"Usually does." He laughs.

His vision pans to Max, shifting his focus from one patient to the next. He places his hand against Max's cheek and lets out a heavy breath.

"This is bad, isn't it?"

Keith manages a warm smile. "It's not completely unexpected, but I would be lying if I said I wasn't hopeful for a better outcome."

At that, Quinn and Wiley walk in, latching the door quietly behind them.

"What's going on?" I ask, scanning the room for information.

"Ask the boss, he called this meeting," Quinn chimes.

"I'll make this quick," Keith begins. "Alex gave us an ultimatum. He said we have forty-eight hours to either leave with him, or he leaves alone."

"That's good, though, to get rid of him?" I ask.

"That was my initial thought, too," he responds. "But then Wiley brought up the thing I hadn't thought of: he knows too much."

A mutual understanding fills the room.

"I'd like to point out my first time being of use," Wiley rejoices.

Keith smacks his arm lightly and mutters, "You know that's not true."

Wiley shrugs.

"Obviously we aren't going with him." His eyes sway to Max, and he continues, "But we can't let him leave, either."

Quinn asks the question the rest of us are thinking. "What are we going to do?"

"I don't know. I'm open to suggestions."

"We could kill him," Wiley submits, matter-of-fact.

A chill creeps through me at a rapid pace.

"That is an option," Keith confirms.

Silence falls, and seconds tick by, filling me with a sad reality of knowing the only suggestion thus far is of killing a man.

"You can't be serious; we can't just kill him," Quinn pleads.

"I'm open to any other alternative that doesn't result in him running back to tell his friends about our location, or worse, that Max's blood saved Skylar."

"Maybe we reason with him? Convince him not to tell them about us," she implores.

Keith shakes his head. "But how do we trust him? That's been the issue the entire time. He's clearly hiding something."

"Then we don't let him leave. We *kidnap* him, lock him up in the cellar until we can figure out what to do next," she says desperately.

"Temporary solution, but I'm not opposed. He's military-trained, incredibly savvy. I doubt we'll be able to get away with it easily, let alone for an extended amount of time," Keith counsels.

"And then we have to consider how pissed he'll be if and when he gets free," I add.

"I guess we'll deal with that bridge when we cross it," Wiley answers, a look on his face I've never seen before.

It makes me wonder what this world has done to him. This world has changed us all, some for the better, some for the worse.

"That settles it," Keith declares. "Unless someone comes up with a better solution, we'll lock him up for the time being."

"How?" I ask

"Leave that to me. No one drink the coffee tomorrow morning."

39

QUINN

I messed up and I don't know how to fix it.

Max still isn't awake, and according to every single bit of math I do, he should have been up by now. The sedation was just supposed to help him sleep, allow him to rest with ease and recharge his body to fight against whatever demon I forced into him.

But that's not the case. The window of time where he should have naturally awoken has passed, and now, I don't know what's happening. I can't help but assume the worst.

On paper it all made sense. His blood reacted against Skylar's, fighting and essentially eliminating the virus. Even the little bit of blood we injected into Skylar had improved her condition slightly, and clearly, the procedure worked for her. But what if we did something wrong, what if we flooded his system too quickly and his body wasn't able to fight back? What was meant to be a rescue has turned into a suicide mission.

I should have never let him talk me into this. I can barely even believe he managed to convince Keith, too, although Keith was heavily intrigued by the scientific part of the whole thing. I know he would never *really* do anything he thought would risk Max's life, but maybe we weren't thinking rationally. Skylar was right when she came to and immediately wanted the procedure to stop. She knew Max was at risk, and we were idiots for continuing, even if we thought it was to help her.

This strange silver lining—a friendship through the heartbreak—stripped away before I could even hold on to it. Don't get me wrong, I'm thankful for the friendship that has blossomed with Skylar, but Max and I grew close these past couple weeks, bonding over shared misery.

"You okay?" Skylar asks, chin resting on her knee while she hugs her legs in the recliner next to Max.

I shake my head.

She continues. "You two were close, weren't you?"

"Not at first." I laugh, remembering how he didn't talk to me at first like he was some feral animal who couldn't be bothered with a human. He was scared, terrified of losing his best friend, the love of his life. It wasn't until he *saw* me, that he could let me in.

"What happened?" Skylar probes, but not in a jealous way, more curious at what she missed kind of way.

"He was lost for a while." I glance at his pale face. "I think he was just so afraid of losing you that he couldn't really comprehend what was happening."

She repositions herself toward me, eager for more.

"He was angry, but justifiably. He didn't know I was helping you. Nearly got into a fistfight with your dad when we put an IV in your arm."

"No way," she says in disbelief.

"Yeah way. We bickered with each other a couple times, and then I don't even know what happened, but one day he snapped out of it and apologized. Thanked me for helping you. Trust me, I was just as shocked as you."

"Wow," she whispers.

"And then we talked. About my past, what happened. We sort of opened up to each other in our time of desperation. He was kind to me, and I felt like he knew, ya know? What it's like to lose someone. I guess that kind of stuff will bring people together. Made me want to fight for you even more." I struggle as the tears do their best to fall, and I do my best to keep them at bay. "I couldn't save Cynthia, but I could save you, and at least one of us wouldn't have to lose the person we loved forever."

"I don't know what to say, Quinn. I really am so sorry."

"I can't help but feel like it will be sort of all for nothing if you end up losing him in the process. I don't mean that to sound as horrible as it does, obviously saving you was so incredibly important, but losing Max wasn't part of the plan, and I have no idea what to do to save him."

A person catches my attention from the door, and when I look up, I see Alex standing in the doorway.

"How's he doing?" Alex asks, sounding more considerate than I expected.

"I don't know."

"May I?" he asks before entering the room completely.

I glance down at Skylar, noticing her stiffen and then standing, her back to Max like she's creating a barrier between him and Alex.

He closes the gap cautiously, standing at the foot of the bed, overseeing Max.

"He looks like crap," he says. "No progress at all?"

"Incredibly minuscule in the grand scheme of things. Steady with no drastic change, but also no deterioration either."

"That's a plus," he adds.

"We're hoping that time helps aid in any type of recovery, but at this point, it's not seeming so great." And just like that, I have an idea. Something that could get Alex out of here alive without him wanting to return for us.

I have to get him out of this room and grab Wiley and Keith for another meeting.

Skylar searches my face, and it worries me that my excitement may be showing too heavily, especially with the context of the conversation.

"I'll leave you to it then." He turns to walk away but then stops to add, "I hope you both know I wish no harm on any of you. I truly am happy that they were able to save you, Skylar, and as much as I disagreed with the things Max did, I would never wish this upon him. He's a good kid, he doesn't deserve this." He says his peace and exits the room.

With a double take to confirm he's gone, Skylar urgently asks, "What the hell was that about? Are you okay?"

"Yes, I just have an idea. A Plan C."

Her eyes widen with intrigue. "What is it?"

"Let's get the guys first. This calls for a meeting."

Maybe it's a stupid idea, maybe it won't work at all. But there's still the chance that it will, and that has to be better than killing a man to keep a secret.

40

———

WILEY

Did I really suggest that we kill a man? Not a deranged man, or a mind-controlled man, but a man who legitimately saved my life and brought me here, to my family, all while risking his own life in the process.

Who have I become?

Part of me thinks that we can trust Alex, not necessarily with the whereabouts of our cabin or Max's blood, but with being who he says he is, and working with a company trying to save us from this mess *The Reformation* caused. But then part of me is worried that Keith is right, and Alex is really some double agent or something crazy and is going to lead us to our deaths.

I am certain that we can't trust him if he leaves. He will undeniably tell his group where we are, what we've been doing, and how vital Max is to helping figure out some kind of cure. There's no way Keith will leave without Max, let alone Skylar or Quinn, and I'm not leaving without any of them, so we're at a standstill. Max doesn't appear to be waking up any time soon, not to mention even if he woke up right this second, he needs to recover before going back out into the world. So that leaves us with the obvious problem we're trying to solve.

Alex can't leave.

There's the first option: we kill him.

But then that leaves us with the whole *we killed a man in cold blood* thing that we will all have to live with for the rest of our lives. It's not like Alex is some horrible man who has caused us pain and suffering or kicked our puppy, he's a genuinely decent person at his core. Conflicted, yes. Difficult, surely. Bossy, absolutely. But he's a good man. And you can't just go killing a good man without doing some kind of damage. But what if that *good man* knows the secret that could potentially put yours and your family's lives in danger? Would that justify ending his life to save yours? How do you even begin to know what the future holds without seeing it through?

The second option is to kidnap him and lock him up in the cellar.

It's not a bad idea; sure, beats killing him. But how are we even going to pull it off? Keith said not to drink the coffee tomorrow, so that has to mean he's going to taint the coffee with a sedative or something to knock him out so we can secure him? Alex is smart; what if he doesn't fall for it? And then there's the chance that he does, and we lock him up. Then what? Eventually, we're going to have to let him go or revert back to option number one: kill him. And at that point, not only do we have murder on our hands, but poisoning, kidnapping, and possibly torture, too.

"Hey," Skylar says, poking her head into Keith's makeshift lab.

Keith looks up from his endless piles of work.

"You two have a second? Quinn has another idea."

Good. Hopefully something better than the seemingly inevitable assassination of Alexander Sanchez.

We walk the picture-frame-lined hallway in silence, filing into Max's bedroom one at a time, Skylar closing the door behind her.

Quinn is smiling, giddy with whatever she's about to say.

"Okay, so," she begins quietly but loud enough for us to hear. "We're worried about Alex telling his friends about Max's blood, right? And that's really the only reason why he would tell them about where we're located, right?"

"Well, they want Keith, too, obviously," I add.

"But they won't want an emotionally distraught Keith," she explains.

Keith scrunches his eyebrows. "I'm not following. Why am I *emotionally distraught?*"

"We fake Max's death." She says the words and then pauses, wide-eyed and waiting for a reaction. No one says anything so she rationalizes, "Okay, I know, it's super morbid, and obviously not what we want to happen in real life, but Alex won't need Max's blood if he thinks Max is dead. He will be of no use to him at that point. And Keith," she points across the room to him, "you'll be in no shape to leave with him, grieving the loss of your son. And clearly, he has no interest in me or you." She points to me. "No offense or anything." She smiles warmly.

I return the gesture, knowing damn well that Alex would rather chop off his legs than take me with him.

"What if he wants proof? What if he wants to see the body?" Keith questions.

"Today when he came in, he asked for permission, which leads me to think he's at least respectful enough to not barge in, especially with you and Skylar losing your shit over his death. We mourn Max and attempt to get Alex out of the house. And the incredibly obvious, we don't have to kill him."

It's not a terrible idea. Definitely not foolproof but ends in not having to kill anyone, at least literally.

"All of this is banking on numerous variables starting with the most obvious, if he'll even buy it. And then whether or not he'll just let me off the hook. He's been adamant about *The Resistance* specifically requesting me. And then, he still knows how to find us, and who knows how many people he'll end up telling. This cabin is our only shot at surviving whatever is happening out there. We have no backup if this cabin becomes compromised."

Skylar chimes in for the first time. "It's not a bad idea."

Keith resumes. "No, it's not a bad idea at all. And I have to admit its lack of committing murder seems appealing. But there are still so many unknowns and what-ifs. Just let me think about it, okay?" He scans the room for any rebuttal. "Let's talk again after dinner."

———

41

ALEX

Days tick by, and with each moment passing, I feel further detached from this group. I didn't expect to be *one of them,* but I hadn't anticipated this. I thought bringing Wiley here would show them good faith, allow them to trust me. I was under the impression we would arrive at the cabin, fill Sinclair in on the details, and then head out, to join *The Resistance.*

I could have never anticipated that they would be this well-off on their own. This place is a prepper's dream; minus the ability to protect them from a nuclear bomb, there are renewable resources to last an indefinite period. The state-of-the-art water filtration system is genius, which runs completely off the grid with stored solar powered energy. I don't know what Keith had in mind when he built this place, but he's prepared for the long haul.

Another thing I hadn't considered is that one of them would have been infected and that another in the group had a blood type capable of bringing her back to life, which according to any and all research I've seen, is impossible.

I didn't realize the group would be so attached to each

other, let alone their precious cabin in the woods. That's what I get for letting my basic human elements slip away again.

People care, people love, people fight for their own.

I was that way once. I cared, I loved deeply, I fought, and I lost; I lost the most important thing in my life and I will forever be changed. Now, I will do everything in my power to defeat the ones who stole my everything.

I inhale deeply, closing my eyes, and with my exhale, I scan the room. A small but cozy spare bedroom I was gifted upon my arrival, where I've since spent most of my time. Wiley opted for the couch in the living room, even though I offered. He had insisted, making a joke about how most of the group has already seen him in his underwear. To be honest, I was grateful for the room, for the privacy, the actually comfortable bed to lay my head. If anything, this has been a pleasant vacation from the shitshow that is life.

An old wooden dresser fills the space next to the bedroom door, laden with photos in frames of smiling faces and trinkets that look like a child made them. The walls are painted a muted lilac, perhaps even grey with a hint of purple. A thick, deep-blue comforter lines the full-sized bed. Everything in the space seems to be mismatched but remains clean, and well kept, like someone preserving an old piece of artwork.

Presently, I sit in a creaky rocking chair in the far corner with a direct line of sight to the door, notebook in hand, preparing an update for my superiors. I continue to struggle with what to write. *Sinclair disregarded the fact that he's one of the best chemical engineers in what's left of the United States, the fact that he could prove useful in helping us all. He would rather stay in his little slice of heaven, with what remains intact of his family.*

It's not exactly like I can say: *His son's blood could be the key to our survival.*

What kind of man would I be, or father that I was, if I threw his son under the bus like that? We don't even know if Max is going to pull through. The procedure never should have worked on Skylar, let alone bring Max back.

I can't put most of this in my report. I'll have to cover it up, only giving bits and pieces. I'll say that I brought Wiley here and Sinclair's group member was infected, she died, and the group refused my persistent offering of safety. But what if they don't buy my story? They know how persuasive I can be, and they know that I know how important Sinclair is. I would be a fool for not dragging him to *The Resistance*.

The other alternative would be to say Wiley died or became infected before we reached his group. That he hadn't given me enough information to find the cabin. That Sinclair is in the wind and that we should move along. But I'd have to come up with a convincing enough story as to how and why Wiley died, because with me, there are no casualties, not unless I intend there to be.

Shuffling footsteps catch my attention from below. They're all funneling into Max's room, closing the door behind them like I don't somehow realize they're having secret little meetings behind my back. I'm the outsider, I get it. I probably wouldn't trust me either.

To give them some space, I grab my gun from off the dresser, holster it, and make my way down the stairs. I open the front door and the warm air from outside welcomes me kindly. I slowly stride down the few steps, landing gently onto the grass below. I inhale deeply, closing my eyes and soaking up the serene nature surrounding me.

Something catches in my hearing, and all of my senses become on high alert.

A thudding, and maybe even grunting.

Almost immediately, I take off in a sprint to the cellar, the sound becoming louder the closer I get. I lift the old weathered hatch and quickly draw my weapon, preparing for the worst. It takes a second for the light to funnel in and my eyes to adjust to the carnage.

The deranged man, pounding his fist into the comatose woman.

He must have somehow gotten loose from his restraints, a task that never should have been assigned to Wiley.

The savage man settles his eyes on me and stops beating the visibly deceased woman. Still in a crouched position, he hobbles on his heels to face me, letting out a low groan. Without giving him a chance to react, I pull the trigger rapidly, one to the chest, another to the head.

His bulky body falls to the floor, and the military man in me recognizes I have to clean up the mess I made.

42

WILEY

I open my mouth to speak but am startled and cut off by the sound of gunshots. Two to be exact.

Keith's eyes widen, and then he speaks. "Girls, stay here." He points in my direction. "You, come with me." He grabs a gun from the nightstand drawer, checking the chamber and then flipping the safety.

With a fluid and cautious motion, he turns the knob, opening the door and using the barrel of the gun to pry it farther open. Cowering behind him, I do my best not to step on his heels, following close. We make quick progress on the first floor and, arriving in the kitchen, Keith snatches a concealed gun from behind a cabinet door.

Extending the gun to me, he says, "Here."

I swallow deeply and wonder why anyone would trust me with one of these things.

I awkwardly take the gun, and he nods like he doesn't somehow know I have no idea what I'm doing. I fake confidence and do the same movements I saw him do only moments earlier.

As I head toward the backdoor, panic starts to rise. There's a level of safety within the cabin and willingly stripping it by going outside doesn't seem much appealing. My heart races, and uncertainty creeps in, sinking its teeth into me.

Keith places his hand on the knob at the same time it moves on its own, Alex bursting through on the other side. Keith raises his gun in a flash and holds it steady while Alex throws up his arms and starts to speak, walking backward slightly.

"Whoa there, it's just me," he retorts.

Keith eyes him suspiciously. "We heard gunshots."

With his arms still in the air and the gun still drawn toward him, he defends, "I went outside, to get out of the house for a bit and heard a noise. Ran to the cellar and found the deranged man beating the comatose woman to death. I had to put him down."

Christ, how did that even happen? I secured him well, but maybe not well enough. I always manage to screw everything up, even the times I'm trying my best not to.

"And the woman?" Keith asks, gun still raised.

"She's dead. She was dead before I got there. I don't know how long he'd been at her."

"Show me." Keith motions with his gun toward the cellar.

"A little courtesy if you don't mind?" Alex nods at the gun.

"Oh, right." Keith lowers the gun but doesn't put it away just yet. He turns to look over his shoulder. "Lock the door behind me. Go let the girls know what's going on. Don't open the door to anyone except me."

"O-okay," I stutter, shutting the door and watching intently while he walks away. Once he's out of eyesight range, I run straight to the bedroom and fill the girls in.

"Holy crap," Skylar mutters. "And you just let him go?"

"Have you ever defied Keith Sinclair? He's more of a do-what-he-says kind of guy."

"True." Quinn snorts.

"Anyway, I'm going to go stand guard by the door, I guess, wait for him to come back."

I head to the kitchen much slower than I made my way to the bedroom, pausing to lean against a barstool during my wait.

Gun still in my hand, I place it gently on the counter to wipe my palms on my jeans. Moments pass, and worry consumes me. What if this is some weird ploy to kidnap Keith? What if Alex knew what we were up to and eliminated the problem like we had tried to eliminate him? What if he's taken him already and will hold him captive until Keith solves the massive epidemic? What the hell would I do without Keith? What will happen to Max? I can't continue to sit here like a bump on a log and do nothing; I have to go after them and make sure he's okay.

With a deep breath, I straighten my posture, picking up the cold, solid gun and take it firmly into my grasp.

A simple twist of the deadbolt and turn of the knob, and I'm outside. The sweetly humid summer air fills my lungs in an instant. Without allowing too much thought, I start my voyage to the cellar. One footstep followed by another, gingerly and fearfully moving toward the unknown.

"Ah, what the hell?" I overhear Keith say angrily.

I pick up my pace, holding the gun out ahead of me, hands trembling. I round the corner and spot Keith and Alex carrying the large deranged man clumsily out of the cellar. Relief floods through me, and I've never been so thankful to see a dead person, or, well, the *right* dead person.

"Just in time," Keith sputters, partially out of breath. "Go grab a shovel."

43

SKYLAR

In the evening, I make my way to the kitchen to find a drink, hoping there is something warm to soothe my aching body. In the chaos of everything, I've managed to push away how I've physically felt, concentrating only on Max. Now that I've spent so much time doing nothing but willing him to wake up, exhaustion fits me like a glove and refuses to let go. Every muscle in me throbs, and my body feels drastically heavier than it should. Not to mention the immense sadness locked inside consuming me that only Max holds the key to.

In the cupboard next to the refrigerator, I locate a few different boxes of tea. Earl Grey, green, and chamomile. I decide on the latter and open two more cupboards before I remember where the mugs are. The white floral oversized mug grabs my attention, but even standing on my tiptoes, I can't seem to reach it.

While retrieving a chair to stand on, Alex walks into the kitchen and offers his help—his long, sturdy arm able to reach the highest section of the cabinet with ease. He hands me the mug.

"Thanks," I say gratefully. "Tea?"

"Sure, yeah. That would be great." He says the words with a hint of sadness lingering.

I'm reminded of how little I know about him.

Once I've filled the kettle and placed it on the stove, I lean against the counter and study Alex. His endlessly dark eyes are piercing, the frown lines between his eyebrows permanently creased.

"So," I say to kill the awkward silence that's formed between us. "You're leaving in the next couple of days?" I watch closely and note how he appears seemingly unfazed by my questioning.

"Yes, ma'am. I need to report back. I hadn't anticipated being gone this long."

"Understandable," I reply, side-eyeing the stovetop to double-check I turned the right burner on. "Do you have a family you're returning to?"

In the slightest, he flinches and regains composure, only a hint of response that most people might not even notice.

"No," is all he says, such a small word that means so little but also so much.

"Everyone tells me you're pretty private, you keep to yourself when you're not busy devising plans and playing superhero."

At this, he laughs faintly. "That pretty much sums me up."

"Hmm, so tell me something about you, something you haven't told the group yet."

His frown line wrinkles itself. "What do you mean?"

"I don't know. I feel like none of us really know anything about you. Tell me something. It could be anything. Your favorite color or favorite food."

He squints like he's trying to find the trick to the question. "Black, and lasagna."

"That wasn't so hard, was it?" I say, offering a smile to ease the tension from his lack of wanting to share personal information.

"Only a little painful," he responds with sarcasm I didn't know he was capable of.

"We're not bad people, you know. We're just all guarded, and it's hard for us to take you at your word when you say so few of them." He doesn't say anything so I continue, "We're all we have left. This tiny group of people, that's it. We're broken and so incredibly screwed up, but we can count on each other and *we* are what matter to one another."

He stares at me for an uncomfortable minute, and I think that maybe he won't say anything else. At last, his mouth opens, speaking quietly, "I lost my wife and daughter."

His declaration stabs me in the heart, and I have to fight back the urge to hug him.

"The um, *The Reformation* took them from me."

I have no idea what that entails but deep down I know it's terrible. The more I learn about this group of people who infected the water supply and caused this epidemic—who managed to nearly kill me and might kill Max—the more I realize how horrific they are.

"They're dead," he confirms.

The kettle on the stove whistles loudly, and for the first few seconds, I don't recognize the sound over the deafening sorrow consuming the room. I make quick work of our tea, chamomile for both of us, and take a seat next to Alex, the tall stool creaking as I get situated.

I struggle to find words, knowing nothing will bring him comfort.

"I'm so sorry, Alex. I don't even know what to say." I trace the handle of the mug with my middle finger and watch the steam rise.

He doesn't look away from the cup of tea in front of him when he says, "I only want to make them pay. I need that."

His proclamation is justified, and when I piece together the minimal yet powerful information, his behavior and demeanor since he arrived becomes much clearer. He's in pain. Alex has essentially shut off his humanity and turned into a robot with one thing on his mind, getting revenge. Here we thought he had some horrible secret like he *was* the bad guy, the puppeteer in control of this nightmare, but in reality he was hiding himself and the trauma he's experienced. The man who is Alexander Sanchez is no villain, he's just broken like the rest of us.

Before I can form any type of response, Keith walks up behind us. I move sideways in my seat and notice his face is twisted in some mix between fear and uncertainty. Immediately my heart seems to drop into my stomach, dissolving into an endless pool of anxiety. I try to catch my breath, and it hitches, and I find myself unable to breathe normally. Alex's eyes widen in response to my labored lungfuls, and his face turns from sadness to worry. He places his large calloused hand on my shoulder.

"Are you okay?"

I open my mouth to speak but am unable to form words. Mentally, I tell myself to stand, but can't seem to get my mind to actually get my body to do what I want. I have to get to Max, something is wrong.

Just when I finally convince my legs to work, my eyes lock on to the cause of Keith's dismay. Like a flash before my eyes, a syringe plunges itself into Alex's totally unaware neck. I gasp, reaching for the impossible, trying to form words, to tell Keith that we don't have to do anything to Alex, that we can trust him, that he's on our side.

But I know it's too late when Alex's eyes bulge, and then

close, his body slumping into his seat, bumping the cup of tea he never even got a chance to take a sip of.

44

———

KEITH

Although I'd like to believe that we could pull off faking Max's death, Alex is too clever for that type of ruse. He would have wanted proof, or a blood sample, or something that would make the whole plan completely useless. I had to divert back to our plan B, locking him up until further notice. Not that it's much of a plan, anyway, given I have no idea what we'll eventually do with him.

Wiley was right, Alex knows too much. He knows things that can compromise our safety and any chance of potential future survival. I couldn't just sit there and let him leave, not if he's clearly hiding something.

Skylar's reaction, although concerning, was the ideal distraction I needed to sneak up on Alex and render him unconscious. I had intended to spike the coffee in the morning, but when I caught a glimpse of the moment he and Skylar were sharing, I seized the opportunity.

"W-what did you do?" Skylar demands through jagged breaths.

"He's okay." I press my fingers to his neck to check for a pulse. I find what I'm looking for and ask, "Are you okay?"

"Is Max okay?" she manages to say while holding her chest, breathing deeply through her nose.

"Yes, well, I mean, no. But there haven't been any changes." I add, "I didn't mean to startle you. I simply saw an opportunity and had to take it."

She starts to calm herself down and she shakes her head. A second passes and she says, "His family."

I don't understand. "What?"

"The, *whatever we're calling them*, they took his family, Keith. They killed them."

I still don't understand.

"He just told me, and Jesus, it explains so much. He lost...everything."

I scan her tired face and then shift my gaze to Alex, his body lying lifeless against the island countertop, his weight slowly sliding off his stool. I grasp his shoulders and position him so he doesn't continue to fall.

My thoughts run wild like a child in a playground, unsure of what to settle on.

"And you believe him?"

Her glassy eyes impale me.

"You can't fake that kind of emotion; the heartbreak he shared with me was very real."

I sigh heavily, now unsure of what to do. I thought I was making the right decision but now I'm not so sure. I only incapacitated him and I would be a fool to think he's going to wake up anything less than pissed off. I should have made a better effort to get him to talk, to get him to confide in me what he did with Skylar. Then maybe I could have persuaded him not to tell his group about us—about Max and what he did for Skylar.

But that's not what happened, and I can't just back out now, I have to follow through with my plan.

"Wiley!" I yell down the hall.

Within a few seconds, his bushy head pops into the hallway, followed by, "What's up, boss?"

"A little help, please."

His eyes focus on the mound of man drooping onto the counter. "What the hell?"

"Help me move him, okay?"

I grab on to the right side of his torso, and Wiley grabs the left. We hoist him slightly and begin to transport him away from his seat.

We're situating his body weight between us when a person commands from across the cabin. "You guys, come quick." Urgency lines Quinn's voice, sending Skylar into a panic immediately and forcing her to burst from her seat and bound across the room.

My worst fear comes to life in the realization that I may have made a terrible choice in using Max to save Skylar, and the consequence will be him leaving me forever.

Wiley's eyes meet mine. "What do we do?"

"Here, let's drop him on the couch," I say in a rush. I move the brunt of Alex's weight as quickly as humanly possible.

His body thuds onto the couch, one arm flinging itself onto the coffee table.

"Keith," Quinn bellows. "Get in here."

I urge my feet to move faster, rounding the corner to Max's bedroom. Upon entry, my heart stops, hand slapping over my mouth in utter disbelief.

I inch closer, blinking back the tears forming, all of the fear since Max fell asleep bubbling up and overflowing.

"You okay?" a tattered voice asks. A flood of emotions pulsates through me.

I had started to convince myself I made a mistake, that the testing I had spent so much time on was wrong, and I had been a fool for thinking this would ever come close to working. Skylar had been saved but at the cost of Max. A bet I never should have wagered.

But, like a wild animal being set free, seeing his eyes flutter open confirmed that we did the right thing, I made the right choice. Skylar was safe, and now, so was Max.

Like slow motion, the scene in front of me unfolds—Quinn begins poking and prodding, asking Max if this hurts or that hurts—Skylar latched on to Max's arm, crying against his side—Wiley standing back, shock and disbelief lining his face.

I soak in my surroundings and the awareness that we're all here, that we're all safe, settles like a soft, warm blanket on a cold winter night. There isn't much I wouldn't do for the group of people crammed tightly in this room. They are my family, all I have left. And I will do anything in my power to protect them, at all costs.

I take a step closer, leaning toward Max. "I'm so glad you're okay." I fight the urge to cry. Suppressing the notion that I might lose him has been a heavy burden to carry. But now that I know he's awake, I feel confident his body will continue to fight the virus surging through his veins. I don't know how close of a call that was, but I know we can't do that again, and I can't let the information of what his blood can do leave this cabin.

My thoughts trail to the living room. Now I have to figure out what to do with Alex.

45

———

MAX

I have no real idea of how much time has passed, but I know I was gone longer than I should have been when I see the reactions of those around me. Their engulfing relief tells a story of concern.

"Come here," I murmur to Skylar while she sobs uncontrollably at my side.

She climbs onto my bed and into my arms, her small body pressing into mine.

"How do you feel?" Quinn asks with her doctor face on.

"Better than I did earlier, that's for sure." Don't get me wrong, I still feel bad; heavy and weighted with a dense cloak of discomfort, but nothing like the impending doom of misery from before I fell asleep. To say I feel better than *that* is an understatement.

I wrap my arms tightly around Skylar.

"I was so worried." She sniffles. "We all were." Her cheeks are red, freckles showing that I didn't know she had.

"How long was I out?" A night, a day, a week, a month?

"Longer than you should have been," Quinn replies.

Wiley grabs on to my hand, squeezing it tightly. "About time you came back, buddy. You had us in a panic."

I glance down at my sides and then touch my face; no feeding tube, no IVs—I couldn't have been out *that* long.

Quinn begins to speak, and when I look at her, really look at her, her drooping eyes seem more tired than I've seen since I've known her. "Can't exactly fake your death now."

"W-what?" I say, startled. "Fake my death?"

"Speaking of that," Wiley interrupts. "Keith TKO'd Alex, so I should probably help him with that."

"TKO'd?" Quinn asks.

"Technical knockout. Don't you watch wrestling?" Wiley jokes and makes his way toward the door.

I shift my face toward Skylar, and she sits up.

"What happened?" I ask.

"Alex gave your dad an ultimatum. Basically said he's leaving and either your dad comes with him or he's leaving alone. Wouldn't be a big deal but, your dad doesn't trust him."

"Trust him with what?"

"You."

"Me?" I say, clearly not understanding.

"Max," she says, bright sapphire eyes meeting mine. "You saved my life. My very *unsavable* life. That's dangerous information."

That's the moment it hits me—Dad is worried that Alex will tell the wrong people, and then my life will be put in danger. But what if I'm somehow the key to stopping whatever is happening to everyone? What kind of person would I be if I blindly disregarded that and went on with my life? Knowing that I could save someone, even if it was one person, isn't something I can just let go.

"What's Dad doing to Alex?" I push my free arm onto the

bed and try to get up, but dizziness takes hold and settles me right back down.

"Not so quick," Quinn orders. "Here, drink this." She hands me a glass filled with a pink-ish drink.

I do what the doctor orders, taking sips of the berry-flavored drink.

Skylar moves herself to the edge of the bed, no longer pressed against my side. The absence of her warmth searing into me, making me ache for her closeness, the security of her comfort.

"Like Wiley said, he knocked him out. Alex had just told me about his family, and your dad managed to sneak up behind him and inject him with something."

"Holy crap," I manage to say between sips.

"Yeah."

"What's he planning on doing? He can't keep him knocked out."

"We sort of agreed to lock him up until we figure out another solution." She avoids my eyes and looks across the room. "It was either that...or kill him."

I nearly choke on my drink.

What the...?

I'm out for a short time and somehow wake to the people I love and trust considering murdering a man in cold blood?

"You're not serious," I ask, trailing my gaze to Skylar and up to Quinn.

She shrugs. "We didn't know what else to do. Trust me, I've been the only one to come up with alternatives to *murder*."

"Can't we just talk to him?"

"That's what I was thinking," Skylar offers. "Listen, he told me his family was killed by the people responsible for all of this." She motions with her hands to the space around us, clearly meaning more than just what's happening in this room. "I think he can be reasoned with."

"Then let's reason with him," I suggest. "We can't kill him. Plus, we need him."

Quinn and Skylar both look at me, perplexed.

Quinn asks, "What do you mean?"

"*The Resistance.* It seems Dad is valuable to them, and if there's any chance at saving the world, we probably need an 'in' with the people going against the man."

I know what I'm saying must sound crazy to them. Putting our faith in this group of people we have no real knowledge of could be a risky move, but so is letting the world fall to shit when we could potentially do something about it.

There are only so many resources here at the cabin, only so much time my dad has bought us by being prepared. No matter how many renewable resources we have, eventually we will run out, and when that day comes, we'll have wished we did more than let a good thing walk out the door.

Maybe it's a stupid move, but maybe it's just dumb enough to be a good idea, like transfusing my blood with Skylar's. We had no real knowledge of whether or not it would work but look at us now—Skylar and I sitting side by side, both alive and decently well. We would have never known this would be the outcome if we hadn't taken that leap of faith. The jump into the abyss with no parachute.

Great things are on the other side of fear, and no matter how much it scares me to put my faith in anyone other than the people in our tight little group, we have to consider the greater good. If we don't think of those other than ourselves, what even is the point of living?

Selfishness gets you nothing but a cruel, unfulfilling and miserably lonely life.

46

SKYLAR

One problem being solved ends up with another problem arising.

Max is awake—something I wasn't so sure I would see happen.

Alex is unconscious—something I didn't expect to happen.

The tears decide to stop flowing, and Quinn, Max, and I decide we need to talk to Keith, and somehow convince him not to hurt Alex. He doesn't trust him, and even though I absolutely understand why, I think he needs to take a step back before he makes another irrational decision.

Even though I would love to spend time with Max, talk about what the future holds for us, it will have to wait for later, when a man's life isn't on the line.

"But I think I should be the one to talk to him. It's me he's concerned about," Max pleads.

"You need to rest." Quinn nods in agreement.

"She's right," she confirms. "Your vitals aren't great yet, and you're still running a bit of a fever. You need to stay put."

"I can't just sit here," he informs, on a mission to sit himself up again, but his muscles are too weak, and he slumps down, disappointment prevalent.

"You can, and it looks like you're going to have to," Quinn says with a smirk.

"Can you at least bring him in here? Let me talk to him, please."

"Okay. I'll try to get him," I offer, even though leaving Max's side is the furthest thing from what I want to be doing.

His lips turn upward, slightly showing the dimples in his cheeks, triggering my heart to do that weird pitter-patter thing you see in the cartoons. I've been so desperate for him to wake up that now I'm overflowing with love.

Without really meaning to, I return the smile.

He voices faintly, "God you're pretty."

My heart thuds again, and the blood rushes to my cheeks.

Quinn smirks and looks up from her clipboard. "You two are gross, get a room."

"You know, *this is* my room." Max grins from ear to ear.

I chuckle and leave, happiness settling comfortably into my body, a euphoric feeling I'm not so sure I've felt in my life.

One foot in front of the other, I make my way to the living room, only to find it empty, couch cushions lying on the floor. Proceeding toward the door, I catch a glimpse of the spilled tea on the counter—such a waste. I head straight to the only other place I assume they would have taken Alex, the cellar. The newly vacant, covered-in-death cellar.

Keith had built it with the intention of it only ever being meant for storms, and the occasional storing of things, but since we've arrived, it's been home to infected people, beaten to death and murdered people, and now a hostage.

The large wooden cellar door is located outside of the cabin, a few feet from the back door, around the side. I lift the creaky, heavy door and gander inside to see Keith and Wiley positioning Alex's body against the wall, a roll of duct tape lying on the floor.

At the same time, they both quickly glance over, eyes wide until they realize it's only me.

I step inside, taking the stairs carefully, one at a time. I'd be lying if I said I wasn't feeling a bit under the weather, the recent events being all sorts of exhausting.

The air is thick and murky down here, and the lighting is grim. The place gives me the creeps, signaling my mind to make a mental note to not go down here alone.

"Hey," I say awkwardly. "If you, ugh, have a minute. Max really wants to talk to you."

I cross my hands and find myself holding on to my arms, cringing while I look around. Cobwebs line the homemade shelf on the wall, stacks of wood below. I trail the room, attention falling on a door on the far side.

"Root cellar," Keith says, startling me.

"What?" I find myself saying in response.

He points to the door. "That's where I store things, like fruits and vegetables."

"Ohh." With each moment passing, I understand more and more how this cabin is set up.

He wipes his hands on his pants and grabs the tape. "Is Max okay?"

"Yeah, I think. He just needs to talk to you." Because he doesn't show any signs of coming, I add, "It's urgent."

He sighs, holding the roll of tape out to Wiley. "Here, can you secure his hands and feet?"

Wiley reluctantly takes the tape and shrugs. "This is a bit extreme, don't you think?"

Keith turns abruptly to Wiley. "Our safety is extreme? Are you going to do it or not?"

"Sorry, yes. I'll do it," he answers sheepishly.

"Come on," Keith urges. "Let's make this quick."

The walk to Max's room is filled with awkward silence and massive amounts of tension. I've never seen Keith this shut off, this cold toward me, and to everyone around. I know he's stressed out, but this is a whole new level of weird, even for him.

When we enter Max's room, he's in the sitting position, propped up with some pillows.

"Dad," he begins in a rush. "Listen, you're overreacting, okay? You don't need to lock Alex up."

Keith shakes his head. "Are you guys serious? *This* is what you want to talk to me about?" He turns to me. "Skylar, you came to get me for *this*?"

I avert my eyes to the floor, the stupidity for being called out scorching like a cattle brand.

"Don't talk to her like that," Max insists, shifting his weight in the bed, another pointless attempt to get up.

Keith rubs his forehead, squeezing his fingers into his temple. "I don't have time for this." He turns in an attempt to make his leave.

Max cuts him off. "What is wrong with you? Why are you being like this? This isn't you."

Without turning around, Keith fumes, "Why am I the only one who cares about our safety?"

"If you care about our safety, then you'll hear me out."

Keith's shoulders slump with another big sigh. "Fine, but please, can you make this quick? I left Wiley in charge and, well, that might not have been the best idea."

47

QUINN

Like a fly on the wall, something I do well, I sit back and watch the drama unfold.

"We need him on our side, Dad," Max stresses.

"Give me one good reason?"

"Other than the fact that he's incredibly useful, a valuable asset to our team, what about the fact that he's our ticket in with *The Resistance?*"

"We don't need *The Resistance.*" Keith taps his foot impatiently.

"We don't? Are you serious? Have you not thought long-term here?"

"Explain," he counters, appearing a bit more interested in Max's train of thought.

Keith leans against the wall, crossing his arms in anticipation. Skylar takes her seat next to Max, looking like she is a queen defending her king—or maybe in an attempt to get away from Keith and his unnecessary rudeness toward her.

"When the food is out, when we have gone as far as possible on supply runs, then what? We have to think long-term. Alex is our long-term. *The Resistance* is our long-term. Trust me, I'm not thrilled about the idea of putting our trust in a stranger, but if he is who he says he is, we need him. We need *The Resistance*. We can only make it on our own for so long, and then we need a backup plan. Clearly, you're of some value to the cause, so maybe we can leverage that to secure our future in this godforsaken world.

"I know you're worried, and I know you think you're doing the right thing, but please consider the words I'm saying to you. Please consider the idea that maybe we shouldn't burn that bridge just yet."

Max's words evaporate into the air as Keith processes the information.

"He knows too much, Max." Keith shakes his head again. "What happens when he tells whoever he works for that your blood can cure a comatose? I know what happens, they take you, they use you as a guinea pig, and they'll have no concern for your life and they'll push it too far. I see it playing out in my head perfectly and I can't allow that to happen. I won't lose you."

They have valid points, and I can entirely see where they're both coming from, but at the end of the day, Keith calls the shots around here, and the fate of Alex isn't looking so great. There are only so many options I can come up with—at least he hasn't killed him yet.

"Then let's talk to him. Can we at least try to reason with him?"

I mentally applaud Max's determination.

"The thing is, he'll tell you what you want to hear, especially now. He's not stupid, he knows how to manipulate."

Max grits his teeth, and Skylar's hand finds its way on top of his in what I assume to be an attempt to calm him down.

"So, you're saying this is a dictatorship then? We get no say in what happens around here?"

I clench my own jaw and study Keith in expectation of his response.

"Why do you care so much?"

"Care? How do you not? You're telling me you're prepared to kill a man because you're afraid? You're going to kill him without even *trying* to reason with him?"

"I never said I was going to kill him," Keith verifies, straightening his posture against the wall.

"How else does this end? You're clearly not going to just let him go. And if you won't talk to him now, then what other alternatives are there?"

Keith's attention falls to the floor like maybe he's finally coming to his senses and realizing Max has a point. "I don't want to kill him."

"Then let's at least exercise all possible options, please." Perhaps finally remembering our existence, he moves somewhat and asks, "What do you girls think?"

Skylar looks to me, and I speak for the both of us. "I think Max could be right." The words come out thick like tar, difficult to speak knowing it's not what Keith wants to hear. Somehow, disappointing him is a harshness I wasn't prepared for.

"Okay," he says defeatedly. "But we all do it together."

———

When Max has finally rested enough to get out of bed, we collectively make our way to the small confines of the cellar. Wiley had informed us that Alex was now awake, and I think that was the final push Max needed to regain what bit of strength was necessary.

I imagine this silent walk to be similar to those experienced in prisons during the time a criminal is about to be executed. Although in this instance, the due diligence has yet to be completed, and death seems an imminent and unjust thing.

We enter the cellar one by one, fanning out and lining the wall opposite Alex. My eyes meet his, and I see a sense of calm I hadn't expected. Perhaps being held hostage isn't new territory to him, or maybe he isn't worried about the outcome, his back against the wall, almost like he's relaxing in his new quarters. An eerie wave flows through the room, and my stomach clenches, filling me full of fear of the unknown.

Alex's mouth opens somewhat, and he begins to speak. "I can only imagine why I'm in here." He holds his duct-taped hands out in front to signify to them. "But I do applaud your efforts, you definitely caught me a bit by surprise."

"I had to seize the opportunity when it presented itself, I'm sure you understand," Keith offers mockingly.

"That I do. It's a great effort, really. I have to ask, though, why?" At this, Alex betrays only partial confusion.

Wiley speaks up. "You know too much."

Like a lightbulb flickering on, Alex confirms, "And you're afraid of what I'll say, and who will find out." He nods. "Understandable."

48

ALEX

"We're at a loss on how to move forward," Keith continues. "Obviously, we can't allow you to leave, and you've made it rather clear you won't be here much longer. And considering the circumstances, we can't exactly go with you, let alone do we trust what our fate would find if we did."

From the other side of the room, Max shifts his weight, allowing the wall to support him while trying to stand tall. He begins, "*We* is a relative term used here." He side-eyes his dad. "*I* would like to have a civil conversation about what's to happen, learn your intentions, and reach a favorable conclusion."

So, if I'm reading this situation right, Keith, in the simplest of terms, wants to bury me out back, but Max is against that, possibly even on my side. They're divided, and cracks like this are what make hostage situations that much more interesting. I don't *want* to manipulate anyone, but taking a small crack like this and shattering it might just be the thing that gets me out of here alive. The next step is to figure out where everyone else stands, find out which hand I need to play.

I shift my eyes from person to person. "And what does everyone else think?"

If my deducing tells me anything, Skylar is probably going to be on Max's side, and Wiley will follow Keith because of their bond, leaving Quinn the odd man out. I could see her siding with Keith because he's the adult here, but she's bonded with both Skylar and Max, not to mention she's pure at heart and wouldn't want to have my blood on her hands.

Skylar shrugs, peeking at Max, and Quinn seems undecided, not really showing any inkling one way or the other.

Wiley contributes. "We just want to hear you out."

"What would you like to know?" I ask this knowing that nothing I say will make Keith trust me, he'll only think that I'm lying.

"Is what Skylar said about your family true?"

The thing that makes me the most human to them—the thing I want to discuss the least—the thing that hurts the most.

It takes me a second to grow the courage to respond. "Yes, what I told Skylar is true."

"What happened?" Keith asks, the question digging in like a knife.

Memories come flooding in, flashes of fear and suffering, and a heartbreak so deep you'd think it would cause actual physical damage.

"I don't know where to start," I say, choking on my speech as it comes out.

"Anywhere would be helpful."

My eyes close, and I breathe deeply, willing myself to say the words, reassuring my mind that just because I say them out loud, doesn't make them happen again. This is the past, and the past can only haunt me so much. Right now, the past seems to be the only thing that can help me.

"*The Reformation*," I volunteer. "They took them."

When I don't say anything else, Keith asks, "What do you mean, they took them?"

More flickers of memories. My daughter's deep-auburn eyes bore into me, bloodshot and full of fear. My wife, fueled with rage, beating against a wall violently.

My voice shakes, and I admit, "They told me it would be okay, that all people on base were to get a vaccine for what was to come. I had meetings to attend, so they went ahead to get their shots. When I finally arrived, whatever they infected them with had taken its hold." I scan the floor in front of me, trying to find something to focus on to will myself not to break in two. "My daughter, Isabel, she...she was fading fast, the virus pulling her under. And Adrienne..." I clamp my duct-taped hands to my mouth. "She was enraged, vicious. Clearly, something was wrong. No one could explain what had happened, but there was nothing that could be done either. They were both gone in a matter of days, and it wasn't until a week later that whispers started spreading that they had used them as guinea pigs to determine the effectiveness of the mind-controlling agents. They had intended me to be one of the recipients, too, but after what had happened, I freaked out. I took the resources I had available and got together with *The Resistance*."

"Jesus," someone mutters barely loud enough to be faintly heard.

Like pleading my case to the jury, I say, "I'm not lying when I say I'm on your side."

"It's not down to what side you're on, Alex, it's what you do with the information you've learned here. This cabin is our only safety from the fallout. And the biggest thing of all is Max. Being a father, you have to understand how I can't just let you leave with the knowledge that Max's blood brought Skylar back to life." Keith's eyes display sadness, a desperate attempt to help me recognize why he can't allow me to leave.

The most humorous part of all is that I never intended to tell them of Max's *special ability*. I would never do that, not knowing the damage it causes him, the risks and potential deadly outcome of ever doing the procedure again. But that doesn't matter because they would never believe me; Keith would never trust that I would keep that locked tight in a vault, never to be spoken.

There's nothing I can say or do to prove to him that I'm not a threat, so I say nothing at all.

49

KEITH

The thought of killing Alex weighs even heavier, knowing this little bit of his past. The one that plays such a huge role in the person that he is.

I am truly devastated for him. The pain I've felt the past few weeks, being so concerned for Wiley, and for Skylar, both of which have been so dear to my family, and then not knowing whether or not Max would make it out alive, is just a blip of what Alex has suffered. I know suffering, having felt it when I lost Maura, the most precious being I've ever known, but to know that her death was caused by anything other than an accident—poor timing and some idiot drunk driver—would be the end of me.

Not only did Alex have to process the loss of his wife and daughter, but he also had to do it knowing what horrible final moments they had, that were caused by a money-grubbing, power-hungry organization.

It's almost like a switch has been flipped, and instead of killing Alex, I have this desperate desire to fight side by side in taking down these people doing such harm.

Max breaks the silence. "If these people are as powerful as they appear to be, we need to stick together. We're all on the same side, and we have to put some faith in each other if we're going to make it out of this thing alive. They've hurt every single one of us." He catches a glimpse at each person in the small space. "We have to stand united, and we have to fight them."

Part of me almost wants to laugh, but not because I think what he's saying is funny, but that my mind is blown how in such a short amount of time he's grown significantly. He's come into his own and become this defiantly selfless human, capable of infinite possibilities. His mother would be proud. He both terrifies me and makes me happy, knowing that he will do the right things in life. Maybe not make the best decisions, given his ridiculous emotions at times, but his intentions are wholesome, and I am so proud of the man he is becoming.

"Kid has a point," Wiley proclaims.

I ask the question that weighs so heavily on my mind. "What happens when *The Resistance* wants to use Max as a guinea pig?"

Alex looks me dead in the eyes. "I know you won't believe me, and I don't blame you for that, but I had no intention of telling them about Max. Not unless I had your permission and knew that he would be safe."

"You're right, I don't believe you."

Alex frowns slightly and then perks right back up. "Go get the logbook from my bedroom. I had written up my briefing, the thing I would be handing in to fill them in on my absence."

At this, I nod to Wiley in hopes that he would understand I want him to go retrieve whatever Alex is referring to.

"Got it, boss," Wiley affirms with two fingers to the forehead and then pointing them at me.

A few silent moments pass, and I ask another nagging question. "What happens if we cut you free? How do I know you won't just kill us all right here right now and take Max with you?"

"I would hope by now you would be a bit of a better judge of my character. I wish none of you any harm."

"I believe him," Quinn opined finally.

I turn my attention to her, and she resumes.

"I thought what happened to Cynthia was just some fluke, some crap luck, but knowing that *someone* is behind all of this, I'm in. After watching Skylar succumb, Max nearly dying bringing her back, I'm ready to make them pay."

"You are my family," Skylar voices quietly. "All of you. If anything, that's something I'd fight for; I'm in."

The tension in the room lifts, and a collective hoorah seems to form. Within another couple minutes, Wiley comes barging in, nearly falling down the stairs.

"Whoops, sorry, lost my footing there." He looks to Alex. "What the hell, man?"

Alex grins, and confusion settles between the rest of us.

"I had to come up with something," Alex says apologetically.

"I'd say so." Wiley laughs.

I give him a look of *what the heck is happening* and he elaborates.

"Alex faked my death in the report, said I died before he ever got any intel of where the infamous Keith Sinclair was. Nothing about Max, Skylar, Quinn, the cabin, nothing."

My eyes widen and my heart swells. Maybe distrusting Alex was the wrong decision all along.

50

———

MAX

My dad is a man set in his ways, certain of his decisions, and typically, it's because he's spot on with doing the right thing. He's wickedly analytical, and problem-solving is what he does best, but somehow, I knew he was doing the wrong thing in regard to Alex. I knew he needed to hear Alex out, to think without emotion and take what the rest of us were saying into consideration.

Granted that over the last few weeks, I saw a completely different side of my dad than I ever knew. I couldn't come to terms with allowing him to become a cold-blooded killer, too.

And now, watching him cut the duct tape from Alex's wrists and ankles, I know that there is a new level of respect between us. He's skeptical, and he's worried, but he put faith in what I had to say, and I'm glad that he finally sees me as an equal, at least enough to change his mind.

"So, what's next?" Wiley asks curiously.

Alex rub's his wrists and stands, surveying Dad for an answer.

"Good question."

"Maybe we should sleep on it?" Quinn suggests.

Dad looks to Alex out of the corner of his eye.

Alex reacts by extending his hand. "I don't fault you for your reaction. I may have done the same, given the circumstance."

Dad stares at Alex's hand before taking it into his and giving it a firm, manly shake.

"Let's sleep on it then," he settles. "It's been one hell of a day, and I think everyone could use some rest. Let's talk about it over pancakes in the morning."

At the sound of pancakes, my stomach growls and Skylar gives me a shy smile. "What can I make you?"

My heart flutters at the sight of her dimples, a calmness settling over me, letting me know that even though everything is massively screwed up, that we might make it out of this okay. And even if we don't, and we go down swinging, at least we have each other.

Skylar was kind enough to satiate my hunger with a grilled cheese sandwich, and when we finish eating, we head back to my bedroom. The space feels so much smaller than it did prior, now that we're both conscious and not being held alive by life support.

"You take the bed." I motion toward it.

"Are you crazy?" she scoffs.

"I'll sleep in the chair, it's okay. I've grown rather fond of that old ratty thing."

"No way in hell you're sleeping in that chair."

"Come here," I say, tugging on her shoulder and bringing her into me. Her hair, a mix of summer and that everlasting scent of lavender, is both intoxicating and soul soothing. Her weight settles against me, relaxing into the embrace. I hold her close and whisper into her ear, "Thank you."

She flinches just slightly in confusion. "For what?"

"For being here. For coming back to me, for not giving up on me."

"I won't give up on you, Max."

She says the words, and they somehow turn into glue, piecing together all the broken pieces of me, giving me hope that I'll be whole again. That no matter what, I'll rise from the ashes, with her by my side. I hold on to her tighter and then gently wrench myself away, placing my hands on each side of her face, staring into her ocean-deep eyes.

"Whatever you need me to be, I will be that. Okay? I don't want to lose you again, not now, not ever. You mean so much to me, you always have, Skylar Morgan. And I don't know if it's the gravitational pull or some kind of invisible string, but I promise you, I will be here for you."

Tears well in her eyes, and just for a second, my heart breaks at the unknown, the possibility that she might reject me —that she might turn and run as far from me as possible. But then she blinks, and a tear rolls down her cheek, and for the slightest moment, she looks to my lips. She stands taller and tugs me down at the same time, déjà vu hitting me as I place my hand on the small of her back, and when we're finally close enough, she presses her angelic lips to mine.

Everything fades away and, in this moment, I know that I am hers and she is mine.

Whatever this world has to offer, we will face it together.

Tonight will be a time for rejoicing and relishing the little moments that impact us the most, and tomorrow, tomorrow we will stand united and take back what is ours, and fight for what has been lost.

ACKNOWLEDGMENTS

Thank you to every single person who supported The Deranged—without you, this book would have never come into fruition.

A huge thank you to my patrons, for monetarily (and morally!) supporting the behind the scenes of writing this book: Victoria, Tyler, The Mask Hunter, Sir Smiles 555, and Christa Stanley. Your support means more to me than you'll ever know.

Emmy Ellis at Studio ENP, thank you for your editing skills.

The entire team at Mibl Art, you are creative geniuses.

Victoria, you get another thank you for your endless support with, yet again, another book.

And to my biggest cheerleader of all, my tiny human. The greatest accomplishment of my life was creating you.

ALSO BY KATE MYERS

The Consequence - Prequel

The Deranged - Book One

The Comatose - Book Two

Want to learn a little more about fan favorite Keith Sinclair? Grab a copy of The Consequence on Amazon, or join Kate's newsletter to get a copy for free!

If you have enjoyed any of Kate's books, please leave a review on Goodreads or Amazon!

ABOUT THE AUTHOR

Kate Myers has been writing fiction since 2013. She obtained a bachelor's degree in accounting and business, only to realize writing was her true passion. Kate does her best writing when she's drowning in coffee and not distracted by cats. She is an avid reader and book lover, young-adult fiction being her favorite to read and write. Kate lives in small-town Ohio. When she's not writing (or reading), you'll probably find her making endless to-do lists that she will either lose or never complete.

Kate also writes new adult paranormal romance under the pen name Luna Pierce, and contemporary romance as Tessa James.

facebook.com/sorryforthekate

instagram.com/katemyersauthor

goodreads.com/sorryforthekate